BLITZ

Railers Legacy 2

———————

RJ SCOTT

V.L. LOCEY

Love Lane Books

Copyright

Blitz (Railers Legacy 2)

Copyright © 2025 RJ Scott, Copyright © 2025 V.L. Locey

Cover design by Meredith Russell, Edited by Sue Laybourn

Published by Love Lane Books Limited

ISBN - 9781785647192

All Rights Reserved

Blitz

When hockey's biggest ego meets football's golden boy, sparks fly, and defenses crumble.

Cole "Trick" Harrington III has made a career out of pretending he doesn't care. Not about his past, his name, or the father who built a megachurch empire off judgment and control. Trick torched every bridge back to Atlanta, deliberately wrecked his career, and buried his truth so deep even he started to forget it. Now traded to the Harrisburg Railers, he's skating on thin ice, with a reputation for arrogance and a career teetering on the edge. The last thing he needs is a PR stunt tying him to a squeaky-clean football star, particularly one who is sexy, strong, and always freaking happy. As Trick is forced to confront his growing attraction and deal with the past he's spent years ignoring—including the younger sister he never knew existed—he realizes that the most brutal battles aren't fought on the ice. They're fought in the heart. And this time, he has to stop running.

Tom Fulkowski has led a charmed life. Starting with a

typical middle-class childhood in Philly, his skill at catching quarterbacks has propelled him to the heights of pro football. He's got the rings, he's got the cash, and he's got the cars. He's also got a bad back, achy knees, and a yearning to move on. With one final season to play with the Philadelphia Pumas before retirement, Tom looks forward to that next phase of his life. He's just not sure what the next phase is exactly. Then, out of the blue, he meets a wild-eyed hockey player with a chip the size of the Liberty Bell on his shoulder. As he and Cole grow closer, he finds a depth to the younger man that resonates deeply. If only Cole would slow down and let Tom catch up to him, they might win it all.

Blitz is an MM romance featuring a bad-boy hockey player with a past he can't outrun, a football legend on the verge of retirement, a forced PR stunt that might turn into something real, and a game-changing journey to their happy-ever-after.

Dedication

*To my family who accepts me and all my foibles and
quirks. Even the plastic banana in my holster.*
VL Locey

Always for my family.
RJ Scott

RAILERS LEGACY

BLITZ

RJ SCOTT
& V.L. LOCEY

Love Lane Books

ONE

Cole Patrick Harrington III AKA "Trick"

I'D BEEN CALLED A LOT OF THINGS IN MY CAREER—COCKY, cold, un-coachable—but this was a new one: Kid.

"Jesus, *kid*!"

"Smile more, *kid*."

"You look like someone pissed in your Wheaties, *kid*."

The man with the camera was talking to me as if I were some fresh-faced rookie and not a twenty-five-year-old professional who'd survived two concussions, a torn MCL, and had cultivated a reputation so toxic even my agent flinched when my name came up. Any minute now, I was going to launch this chirpy, caffeine-fueled photographer from the top floor of the Railers practice facility and act as if it was a training accident.

I gritted my teeth and resisted the urge to lose my shit, mostly because I'd been warned—again—that this PR stunt was a chance for me to play nice. Apparently, how I got myself traded from Atlanta had been way too effective. I may have overplayed my hand at my old team when I tried my hardest to make myself the bad guy to escape the specters that loomed large in Georgia. The Railers had scooped me up like a clearance-sale gamble, hoping maybe a change of scenery would fix whatever was wrong with me—as if I was just some glitchy piece of tech needing a reboot. But instead of skating drills or hitting the weights to prove I still had game, I was stuck posing with a golden-boy football player in a sponsored shoot for BoltFuel—oiled up, half naked with shorts the only thing hiding skin, and gritting my teeth while trying not to explode at everyone in sight.

Worth it to get out of my dad's way. Right?

"We are smiling," Tom said beside me, his voice bright enough to make my teeth ache as he elbowed me with what I assumed was solidarity.

His default setting was probably grin-and-glow, the kind of guy who thought the world could be fixed with a good attitude and an extra scoop of protein powder. He wasn't only smiling—he was radiating PR-friendly charm as if it was his job. And maybe it was. Meanwhile, I was trying not to set the BoltFuel banner on fire with my eyes.

"This way, Trip! Smolder for me, Trip! Love that protein drink, Trip!" the camera guy shouted.

"It's Trick," I corrected. Everyone wanted to call me Trip for the III, but no, I was Cole *Patrick* Harrington, and people had better remember that it was Trick from Patrick.

My dad was Cole Harrington—Pastor Cole—slick with charm, polished by the spotlight of his Temple of the Radiant Truth ministry, and backed by generations of old Southern money.

"Trick, then. Smile!"

According to Layton Foxx, the Railers PR guru,

sunshine-football-guy and I were good for BoltFuel, the team, and hell, even the league. I was surprised he didn't tell me it would lead to world peace, but apparently, the optics were perfect: hockey's most controversial problem child standing next to football's favorite son. I gritted my teeth and forced my trademark golden-boy grin. This was good for image and cross-market promotion, and excellent for a company trying to prove their product wasn't just for gym bros and weekend warriors.

BoltFuel's directive had been front and center in the email thread leading up to this shoot—***DON'T LET HARRINGTON FUCK IT UP FOR US.*** All caps. Bolded. Message received loud and clear. Be good, be agreeable, and sell the shake. Keep your attitude on a leash and your mouth shut. That was all they needed from me: a warm body and a winning smile.

The camera flashed, and I clenched my fists, digging my nails into my palms. I focused on my breathing, slow and controlled. One… two… three. My jaw ached from clenching, and my shoulders were so tight my head hurt. Ten seconds of pretending. Ten seconds of not messing up in front of BoltFuel, the team, and the one guy in the room who seemed untouched by the circus. Ten seconds of being someone I wasn't—I could do that. Hell, I did it every day.

Tom I'm-fucking-perfect Fulkowski, carved out of golden light, good intentions, and twenty million a year, stood beside me as though he didn't have a care in the world, flashing his perfectly white teeth and charming everyone from the interns to the assistant GM. He even smelled good, like sunshine and cinnamon. I smelled like sweat and frustration.

We both smelled of oil.

Taller than me by a couple of inches, he was broad-shouldered and stupidly photogenic. He wore his Philadelphia Pumas shorts as if he belonged in a magazine ad instead of a football stadium.

"Trick? A word," Layton said from the sidelines, all pleasant PR charm until I got closer, and he pulled me aside like a cop about to read me my rights.

"What! I'm doing it! I'm smiling, aren't I? I didn't swear, flip anyone off, or smash a camera. That's practically sainthood."

God, it was hard to turn off the asshole side of me.

"I swear, Trick, if you don't pull it together and act like you're even vaguely enjoying yourself, I will *personally* staple that BoltFuel logo to your forehead. This campaign is already hanging by a thread, and if you tank it, you're not just screwing yourself—you're screwing me, the team, and everyone who still thinks there's a PR miracle waiting to happen here."

Message received. Loud and clear. Again.

"Act like you're happy we plucked you off the waiver wire. Smile, nod, and for the love of god, Trick, look like you're thrilled to be standing next to America's sweetheart and holding a protein shake like it's your golden ticket back into hockey heaven."

I crossed my arms over my chest, letting the PR-approved smile drop like dead weight. I didn't want to be told what to do. I'd escaped Atlanta to be my own man, and here was this guy shouting at me.

"Even if I'm not happy?" My voice was flat; the kind of tone that said I was two seconds from lighting the whole BoltFuel banner on fire to see who'd scramble first.

Layton's eyes darkened, and I could see the vein in his temple starting to throb. "I swear…" he began. "Do your job and pretend you want to be part of the Railers." Then, he gently encouraged me, aka shoved me, back out onto the rooftop where Perfect-Tom-the-football player was chatting to the photographer and smiling so damn hard I was surprised his face didn't break.

"Here he is," Tom said, throwing me the same smile.

Fuck. My. Life. Happy to be with the Railers? I wish. After the reputation I had—the one I'd created to escape— no one *really* wanted me here. Hell, I didn't want to be in Pennsylvania—I'd wanted Vancouver or LA—anything to get as far away from Atlanta as possible.

I need to try and smile. I need to look unaffected. But I need to smile.

My head!

Tom leaned in. "You good, dude?"

Dude? Who the fuck said that anymore? And no, I wasn't good. I hadn't been good in years.

"Peachy," I muttered, forcing a tight smile for the next shot. The camera clicked again, and I caught sight of my expression on the monitor. Yeah. Real sunshine and rainbows.

"Okay to post to my socials?" Sunshine asked.

The photographer nodded, and before I knew it I was being hugged super close, skin on skin, and Tom's phone caught my automatic media smile before I extricated myself and made a show of wiping myself down.

"So, onto the interview," the camera guy said, standing

aside for the slip of a girl who couldn't have been a day over eighteen. The questions were generic. Layton wanted us to banter about hockey vs. football, even after I pointed out that I was earning seven million a year, which was less than half of what Sunshine-Tom pulled in. Was that the banter he wanted me to focus on?

Tom was chatting about the many charities he was involved with, from dogs to kids to mental health. He was all over everything: fun runs, ultra marathons, kicking balls through holes.

"... charities?" the interviewer asked, looking at me expectantly.

"I prefer to keep my charitable endeavors private," I threw out, rude as fuck, and pointedly raising an eyebrow. Why the hell did I do that? Oh yeah, because I didn't do charity work. I gave half my freaking salary to my dad.

Silence. I could feel Layton's gaze boring into the back of my neck. "Apart from the dogs," I added after a pause. "I do a lot with dogs." I wondered if anyone could tell I was lying. Again, no one would call me on it, and I resolved to donate to the closest dog rescue place.

"You do?" Tom asked, "That's so cool. I love dogs! I have this cute pup... look!" He'd picked up his cell and was now waving it under my nose.

I was motion sick but managed to at least murmur something that got him to stop waving it at me.

When the interview was over, I was free to leave, but Tom wouldn't let me. Oh no, he wanted to talk to me.

"Do you want to get a coffee?" he asked with a grin, as if we were old friends and not two strangers thrown together for a PR campaign no one had asked for.

Did I want to spend time with another man—a gorgeous, sexy, muscled, oiled man—where my urges might spill over and I did something stupid.

Nope.

Don't look at his body. Mask down.

Scrappy miserable defensive shield up.

"Why? So, you can add rehabbing hockey player to your list of charity cases?"

He didn't flinch, but he did frown. "Just an idea," he said. "No biggie."

Anyone would notice Tom the second he walked into a room. He was tall and had a lean, but powerful, football player's build—one of the top defensive ends in the league. He was clean-cut American perfection, with hair cropped short and neat, blue eyes that probably melted cameras, and a jawline sharp enough to cut glass.

He turned slightly to talk to the photographer, and the view from the back didn't disappoint. Broad shoulders tapered down to a narrow waist, and his ass—well, it was ridiculous in those Pumas shorts. That was some fine award-winning bubble butt he had going on there. His whole body looked as if it had been designed in a lab to torment me.

And those lips—Christ. Full, plush, shaped like sin and confidence. The kind of lips that made you think of things a man shouldn't, especially in front of half a dozen cameras. I could imagine tracing them with my fingers, feeling them against my neck, and yeah… his lips would be gorgeous wrapped around my—

My cell buzzing interrupted my thoughts—not my normal cell phone, but the tiny handset I kept tucked in a zipped pocket of my bag. It only had one number programmed into it. My father's.

I didn't want that man anywhere near the real life I was trying to build. He didn't deserve even the ghost of a presence in it. Everything I'd clawed my way toward—every minute on the ice, every hard-earned scrap of control over my own goddamn story—I'd done in spite of him. Not because of him.

But I couldn't make myself leave the phone behind. Not ever. Because I knew him. Knew the way he operated. He'd wait until the perfect moment—until I was almost happy, until I was steady—and then, he'd throw a curveball that'd knock me sideways. He'd done it before. Enough times that the idea of missing one of those calls, of not being ready, left a knot of barbed wire in my gut.

The phone was my warning system. My fire alarm. I didn't pick it up to talk. I picked it up to survive.

The message was simple. A lone photo, forwarded from Tom's Instagram. His arm slung casually around me, my head tipped slightly toward his. It wasn't anything.

Below it, my father had typed: *The cameras have caught you touching sin!*

My stomach dropped.

Classic him. No context. No conversation. Just a warning dressed up as scripture, like he thought he was standing at a pulpit instead of slinging shame over text. Like he had any right to say a damn thing about my life after our contract.

I stared at the message, my grip tightening on the tiny phone until the plastic creaked. This was the curveball. I'd felt it coming. He always found a way to remind me that he was watching.

"Trick! Security just called," someone said, cutting through my spiral. Now what? "There's someone downstairs for you."

"Who?"

"Don't know. Greg said it's personal."

I blinked, heart thudding as if I'd been caught doing something illegal. I turned back to the photographer. I was thankful for the interruption, even if my chest was tight—I didn't do anything personally. "Are we done here?"

He nodded, distracted by adjusting some lighting rig.

I didn't say goodbye. I shoved my hands deeper into my hoodie pockets and walked off the set without glancing back, using the stairs to get down, and stopped just before exiting the lobby. My breath hitched and my heart punched against my ribs as if it were trying to escape. Panic curled in my gut, sharp and sudden, coiled tight like a spring ready to snap. My palms were slick, my vision narrowing as thoughts raced—who was out there wanting me? Did they want a golden boy hockey player or an asshole wanting to be punched? What character would I have to play? Not knowing was kinda shit, and I didn't do surprises. Tension flooded my veins, thick and hot, locking up every joint until I couldn't move or think without spiraling into worst-case scenarios.

"Hey, you okay?" a voice said behind me, and I whirled to face a half-smiling, half-concerned Tom.

I focused on his stupidly pretty face and sneered. "Oh, fuck the hell off," I snapped, and pushed out of the door, my anger at being spotted enough to snap my daydream. I didn't think he followed me, and I strode to the main desk, seeing an empty lobby apart from some kid sitting on the sofa.

"What?" I asked Greg, who pointed at the young girl without saying a word. "We don't let fans in."." I moved to leave, but the girl had moved—damned fast—and blocked my way.

She couldn't have been more than seventeen, eighteen maybe—but then, what the hell did I know—and she smiled up at me. She was in jeans and a simple T-shirt, the kind you could pick up in a three-pack at Target, and her hair was scraped back into a no-nonsense ponytail. There was no makeup I could see, but she didn't seem plain— just real. Her dark eyes were wide, curious, and maybe a little nervous, like she wasn't sure if she was about to get yelled at or hugged. There was something familiar in how she stood too—shoulders back, chin lifted as if she'd practiced this moment in the mirror a dozen times and wasn't about to flinch now.

"Hi, Cole Harrington *the Third*." She extended her hand to shake.

I ignored it.

"You shouldn't be in here; there are scheduled times for meet and greets," I said. "Give Greg your name, and he'll add you to the list." I stepped back so Greg could see her and me in case I got accused of something awful; I mean, Jesus, she was a young woman, and I was the bad boy of hockey, and I'd been accused of unfounded shit before.

"My name is Rebecca Jensen."

"Okay. Tell Greg."

"I'm here to see you."

"As I said, we have meet and greets."

"I'm your sister."

"Fuck off." My mouth moved before my brain could catch up. Sister? No. That word didn't belong to me. That word wasn't part of my life. My entire world had always been me—solo, closed off, self-contained. No siblings, shared birthdays, hand-me-downs, or late-night whisper fights across a hallway. Just me and the silence I'd made peace with. And now? This stranger wanted to rewrite my entire history with a few words. That was a new one. I'd had four pregnancy accusations—two of them from women I'd never even met, one from a former one-night stand who'd forgotten she was married, and one who thought wishful thinking made it real. I'd punched a photographer in Vegas after he'd tried to shove a lens up my nose during a hangover. I'd been accused twice of getting too handsy in public—both dismissed, but the stain lingered. I'd been called every name in the book by commentators and sports pundits alike. But this? A long-lost sibling showing up out of the blue in the Railers lobby? That was a first.

"No, you're not," I scoffed. If there's one certainty I have, it's that I don't have siblings. "Greg, can you get over here and deal with this."

"Cole Harrington, the second, was your father, same as mine," she said, her voice steady, like she'd rehearsed this a hundred times. "My mom, Georgie Jensen, was your dad's PA for a couple of weeks. She never told me about him—not until last year when she was diagnosed with cancer." She paused then, grief in her expression. "She told me to stay away, that it was safer that way, until I turned eighteen at least. And I'm eighteen now, I mean... look, when she passed away there was a lawyer explaining everything."

She reached into her bag and pulled out an envelope, which was thick and official judging by its weight. "There's a genetic match, an affidavit, photos... the whole kit and caboodle." Then, she smiled—wide and awkward —and added, "Hey, big brother."

"Is this a scam? Because if it is, save us both the time and get the hell out now. I've seen enough people try to angle in with a sob story and some paperwork. You want money—there's a line forming behind my last three fake cousins and a guy who swore he babysat me once in kindergarten and said I told him my dad would give him money. So, unless you've got more than a manila envelope and a smile, I suggest you turn around."

"She said you'd be like this," she muttered, then sighed. "Take this, asshole." She thrust the envelope at me. "Call me."

Then she turned smartly on her heel and walked out of the arena, leaving me in the lobby like an idiot. An idiot holding a sealed envelope and a hundred questions I didn't want to ask. My fingers itched to tear it open, but my feet stayed rooted to the floor. What the hell was I supposed to do with this? What if she was right?

She's not right. Jesus Trick, pull yourself together.

I shoved the envelope into my hoodie pocket as if it

were radioactive. Greg was staring, and I snarled. He scampered off to do whatever he was supposed to be doing, like not letting a random stranger in here.

This day was officially fucked.

TWO

Tom

TRAINING CAMP.

Two words that held great promise for a team. New beginnings. Fresh dreams realized. Camaraderie. Bonding. Preparing for the agony and ecstasy of a new season just over the horizon. Hungry rookies hoping to secure a spot on the roster. Seasoned vets working to keep their positions locked down. And then, there was the grizzled old man praying his fucking knees held out for one last chance to lock lips with the Vince Lombardi Trophy.

That was me. Thirty-three, but still a grizzled old man dreaming of one last tango with that gorgeous silver prize before sailing off into the sunset. Yeah, the dream was nice. The reality of the Pumas getting all those accolades? Time would tell. We'd managed to claw our way into a playoff position in the NFC East last year only to be knocked out by those cocky shits from New York.

If I laid real still in bed, like now, and closed my eyes, I could still see that fucker in the red and blue streaking past me to pick up a crucial first down leading to a touchdown that won that game for New York. Many a person—person meaning fans and sports journalists—had said it was time for old Tom Fulkowski to hang up his cleats. Emphasis on the *old* part.

To the rest of the world, thirty-three is still young. In football? Not so much. Most pro football players retire from the sport between thirty-four and thirty-six. Some stay longer, mostly quarterbacks who aren't subjected to the punishment that linesmen … are…unless they are in my sights, then down they go. Sorry not sorry.

Contact sport is not kind to the body. Ask my knees, my shoulder, and my noggin. We won't talk about the concussion two years ago, or the one five years before that, or the two I'd gotten playing for Ohio State way back. Nope. We weren't going to think about that shit because it would depress me and, hey, it was opening day of training camp for the Philadelphia Pumas! Rah-Rah-Shit-My-Knee-Aches. I rolled to the side of my big, empty bed to see what appeared to be fog outside my window but was actually thick, hot, gross summer air. Oh joy.

Yay. Nothing added to the merriment of speed drills; agility, strength and endurance tests; and the always deeply loved medical and psychometric tests like ten thousand percent humidity. The feel of a soaking wet cup cradling your drenched, saggy balls was always enjoyable.

Blah. I needed to shake off this mindset. A new day had arrived, and with it, new adventures to… uhm, new adventures to adventure into.

"Okay, Tommy, rise and shine. Let's show those youngsters how the old guy charges the quarterback."

No one replied other than Winnie, my black cocker

spaniel, who, upon hearing my voice, leaped from her bed on the floor to mine. She bathed my face with kisses as I smiled.

"And then one more year and I'll be out and proud." I told her.

No one in my professional career other than Tyrese knew about my sexuality, and our starting quarterback-slash-my-best friend would keep my secret. Only one more year. Then, I could come out, date men freely, and maybe find someone to settle down with. I had this big ass mansion, cars, money, and a charming smile, according to everyone that met me. I was kind, easygoing, and cheerful. Also, not to brag, but I had a pretty nice body for a man my age, and my dick was nice. Sure, all men thought that, but the few elite escorts I had hired on occasion had complimented my dick. Were they just saying that to boost my ego? Get a bigger tip? Maybe. But my dick *was* pretty nice.

"Winifred, why am I lying here complimenting my own penis?" I asked the dog while she snuffled my face.

She yipped, and that got me going. The dog streaked from the bed and out of the bedroom door making a beeline to the back door. I sat up slowly, threw my big feet to the floor, and gave my bones a stretch. One in my neck popped so loudly I winced. "Shit, is that supposed to do that?"

No one answered. Heaving a sigh, I rose, found my robe, and made my way through my four bedroom, seven bath, eight thousand square foot home in Cherry Hill. It had everything—from the grand arched portico to a five-car detached garage to an in-ground pool and tennis court, and a gaming room. White oak entryway, skylights, coffered ceilings downstairs, a chef's kitchen for my private chef, Jonny Mash, and a full two acres of fenced-in privacy. It was a gorgeous place. And it was equally lonesome.

"Just one more year, Tom. Then, we're hitting that soulmate search hard," I told myself as I passed my personal gym and padded down the stairs. Winnie was doing a pee dance at the back door when I finally got there. Why did I have such a damn big place when it was just me and my dog? "Okay, just cross your legs for another minute."

I jogged through the laundry room, tidy as a pin because my housekeeper, Mona, would not have it any other way, and tapped the disarm button on the security panel before I unlocked the doggie door. Winnie bolted out of the little panel. I stepped outside in my robe to breathe in the glory of August in Philly deeply into my lungs. Man, it was sticky. Only six a.m. and the humidity was atrocious. I couldn't wait to get to the Hillerman Care Complex in South Philly and start running drills. The sports complex where the Pumas held camp was state-of-the art. The dorms were posh, the gyms and medical facilities top-notch, and the practice fields perfectly manicured. But there was no escaping the dog days when you were out in the blazing sun.

The air was thick and moist. I play-gagged, then went back inside to whip up a protein shake to start the day. Jonny was on leave due to me being at the Hill—what we called the training complex—for the next five weeks. Mona would come in to dust during that time, but otherwise, the house was empty, which was nothing new. As I dumped my powder into some cold skim milk and tossed in some bananas, I flipped the blender on and let my mind wander. It danced back to that touchy hockey player at the energy drink shoot the other day. BoltFuel had not warned me that the dude I was doing these promos with would be so hot. Nor had my agent. A heads-up would have been nice, but then again, no one other than Tyrese knew I was into jocks with attitudes. No twinks for me. I liked a guy I could wrestle around with and not worry about hurting. Trick looked solid. As though he could take being tossed onto the bed and covered by a defensive end intent on licking that bubble butt of his. I'd not just stop at his ass either. I'd work my way up his lean but hard body, paying particular attention to his dick as it wept and—

"Hey, you awake?" Tyrese bellowed from the foyer.

I hurried to shove at my semi and get it hidden—I hoped—in the folds of my robe. Ty had the code for the front gate, the doors, and even had a spare key. I hurried to turn off my well-blended shake as he entered the kitchen. Ty was the epitome of everything masculine. Tall, strong, possessing great leadership skills. He was a beautiful Black man on the cusp of immortality in football. Future Hall of Famer for sure, he simply needed the Pumas to help get him that fat gold Super Bowl ring for his finger. And he would, I was sure of that. Before he hit thirty. Whether I would be here to see that happen for my best friend, I didn't know, but I sure as hell hoped so. "Why are you still in your grandpa robe?"

I glanced down at the soft, thin flannel robe that had been washed so often the plaid design was barely there.

Mona threatened to throw it out weekly but, so far, it had survived the purge. Thankfully, I was behind the island, so my hard-on was out of sight.

"I'm having a shake." I told him, because that was how we did things. I held up the pitcher. "Shake. Which was part of the noise you heard and followed to find me."

He rolled his dark brown eyes, then went to the glass cupboard to get himself a tumbler. I poured him half the shake. We toasted each other, then downed the vanilla-banana delight. Ty made a face. He was not a fan of the banana.

"You are going to start oozing banana from your pores," he warned as Winnie came charging in to do a pet-me dance on Ty's slick gold Italian sneakers. "Is that some of that taste-test shit from BoltFuel?"

"Yeah, it's pretty good. They're setting up for a huge push for sports drinks and protein shakes for athletes that they're hoping will take off. They gave me cases of all their products to try since I don't endorse something that I don't like. The stuff is really good. They got this tagline about "no matter what your sport BoltFuel will energize you." Which is why they had me shoot some stuff with a hockey player from Harrisburg."

He glanced up from rubbing Winnie's belly. She adored Ty. Most women did. "Is it all banana-flavored?"

"No, I added the bananas. They have a ton of flavors. Grab a container from the pantry. Ty nodded, then returned to fussing over Winnie. "Give me ten to shower and get my bags. Then, we'll take Winnie to Paula's. Then, you and she can kiss goodbye."

"Me and Winnie?" he teased.

"No, you dork, you and your girlfriend."

I loved Paula so much. She was not only the winner of last year's Miss Black Philadelphia Beauty Pageant she was also in her final year of law at Drexel University. Smart, stunningly pretty, and with a sense of humor that never failed to make me chuckle. I'd never had a sister— only three step-brothers—so I claimed her as my sibling. She was happy to have a big, pasty man as her adopted brother.

I was out the door with my dog in fifteen. No point to making myself look good for the trip to her apartment complex overlooking the Delaware River. We got Winnie situated, got Ty kissed a few dozen times, and got myself a loaf of banana bread still warm from Paula's oven.

"Why didn't I get bread?" Ty asked as we made our way to the training facility.

I stuffed bread into my face, smiling at him the entire time. "She likes me better."

"Oh, I doubt that. She calls you pasty."

"I am pasty. Have you seen my belly?" I reached down to tug my tee up and there it was. Toned, sculpted, but definitely pasty.

"Jesus, cover that up!" he exclaimed as we slowed to enter traffic. "I've never seen a man so devoid of pigment."

"I have some, just not much. It's my Slavic genes. Look it up." I covered my belly after dusting off some stray crumbs. "My question to you is, when are you going to marry the woman who made this bread? If I were straight, I'd arm wrestle you for her."

"She's not ready," he said, merging into a slow-moving

morass of cars. "I keep bringing it up, but she wants to finish law school first and get set up in a good practice."

"That makes sense." I chewed and contemplated. "I'd like to get married someday. Maybe even have a kid. Just one. No more than two." Ty glanced at me as we sat at a red light. "What?"

"Maybe if you came out, you could find that right guy. I know, I know, it's hard, but shit, Tom, you wouldn't be the first."

"I know. Thanks, Ty; I love you."

"You're just saying that because my girl bakes that damn nasty bread for you."

"And watches my dog."

"*And* watches your dog." He flashed that smile that made all the ladies swoon. Some of the men too, for sure.

I chewed as we crept along towards Center City. I knew all of what he said was true. It seemed easier to do it after I was done playing with pigskins. While the league liked to brag about how inclusive it was, locker rooms told a different story. I heard the whispered slurs when the players thought management couldn't hear them. Not all of the players. Obviously. Just a few, but those few were dogged in their bigotry. I had one season left on my contract. Unless I met someone who really knocked me for a loop, I'd keep my head down, retire, and then, post a picture of me and my bae watching the sun set from a romantic tropical paradise. Maybe that made me a coward. Probably so. But right now, all I wanted was to go out with a fucking bang this season. And that meant eye on the prize and no stupid romantic entanglements.

Easy. Peasy. Banana bread squeezy.

I could do that. Not like the paid companions I rarely used would be looking for domesticity. I could live another year alone. There was no one on my radar that I would risk my final year in the league for. Other than Trick the hockey player, I'd not met anyone who pinged my interest. But he was over two hours away. Not that it was a great distance. He wasn't playing hockey in Russia or anything...

"You ever watch hockey?" I asked around a bite of my third slice of banana bread.

Ty chuckled. "Nah man. I've never really watched it much. I know there's ice and sticks and they all seem to be missing teeth."

"Not all of them." I picked a raisin out of the half loaf sitting on my lap, the foil torn asunder as if a hyena had dived into the baked goods, then tossed it into my maw. "Some of them have all their teeth, they just don't show them much. We should go sometime."

"Yeah, we can do that." He, then, began chattering away about some wiener dog on the internet that played goalie. Ty enjoyed silly animal videos.

My thoughts went back to Trick. He probably looked even better when he smiled, but I'd not seen a smirk or the twitch of a real smile that whole shoot. Maybe he needed someone to crack a few jokes, loosen him up a little. Maybe I needed to stop this right now. Trick was more than likely as straight as Ty and not searching for some elderly DE to come shuffling into his life or bedroom. Still, he *did* seem like he needed someone to cheer him up, and I was incredibly good at that. Almost as good as I was at knocking quarterbacks on their asses.

THREE

Trick

MY AUGUST WAS FUCKING BULLSHIT. IT WAS GETTING TO know the Railers; it was pretending to be fucking happy and dealing with having a potential sister bullshit.

"It's bullshit," I told my rental. "Fucking bullshit," I explained in the shower to my shampoo. It was a nice shower in a nice rental decorated in a nice style with nice sofas and a nice kitchen in a nice neighborhood. "And it's all bullshit."

Naked in my bedroom, letting it all hang out to give me some natural drying time, I studied my clothes, searching for the least bullshit outfit I could wear to yet another Railers barbecue at which I was supposed to forge a lifelong bond with my fellow skaters as we headed into pre-season.

"Lifelong my ass," I snapped and yanked jeans and a T-shirt out of the closet. It was only as I was tugging the T-shirt over my head that I realized it was Atlanta Phantoms' colors, with my freaking number on the back. "Shitting fucking bullshit," I muttered and tore it off like it was burning my skin, then sagged to the bed, hollowed out. Just like that worn faded T-shirt—discarded and pointless.

Thoughts of the girl at the rink wouldn't leave me alone. The envelope she'd handed me, the way her eyes looked so damn hopeful—as if she already knew the answer. Rebecca Jensen.

My sister?

A sister. For fuck's sake.

I yanked the Pastor-Cole-only phone out of my pocket, heart hammering. I didn't let myself think twice. I hit call before I could talk myself out of it.

"Do I have a sister?"

Silence.

Not bad reception silence. Deliberate silence. The kind he used as a weapon. The kind that came right before the sermon.

Then, finally, his voice—smooth, graveled, soaked in righteous indignation. "Our lawyers are dealing with it."

"Do. I. Have. A. Sister?"

"I said our lawyers are handling it. She's a liar, a con woman. She just wants your money."

I laughed, sharp and bitter. "Bit like you then."

That hit. I heard it. But he recovered fast. "Watch your tone," he thundered, voice booming as if he thought he was still preaching from the pulpit. "You are being tested, Cole. Temptation comes in many forms, and Satan often wears the face of family. The girl is not your sister. She is a distraction. A snare. Her entire story reeks of manipulation, and you are letting your flesh guide you instead of your faith."

"My what?"

"This is what happens when you step outside the light. When you abandon your purpose. I raised you to be a warrior of the Word, not a slave to lies. If you let her in—if you believe her—you shame your mother's memory. You shame me."

"Good," I snapped. "Because you've never once made me proud to be your fucking son."

The silence that followed wasn't righteous anymore. It was ice-cold.

Then, the line went dead.

My hands were shaking, and fury rose hot and fast—like it always did with him. I wanted to throw the phone. Crush it. Slam it into the wall until it cracked in half, until there was nothing left of the connection between us. But I didn't. I sat there, staring at the plastic as if it had personally betrayed me.

Because what would it change?

If she was my sister—if he was her father by blood—then that didn't fit in to his version of the truth and was a crack in the perfect lie he'd built.

And I'd fallen right into the trap. Let him in my head again. Let him flip the switch, tear up the floor under my feet like he always fucking did.

My fists loosened and my shoulders dropped.

I hated him.

But I couldn't go against him.

I caught sight of myself in the full-length mirror, thick skater thighs stretching denim, honest-to-god six-pack, sinful cum gutters, nipples perfect, a slight dusting of dark hair, broad shoulders, muscled arms, but it wasn't all the good stuff I was staring at, it was my miserable face. I should've been happy—I wasn't in Atlanta anymore. I was free.

"Smile," I ordered and watched as my muscles twisted into a weird-ass grimace, and I closed my eyes.

Breathe.

Atlanta management had traded me as I'd asked—but then, I'd planted so much on social media and messed up so badly last year, it was an easy sell—anything to get out of Georgia, but of all the teams in the league, why the Rainbow Railers? Dad had been pissed. He'd given me a full-throttle lecture about the sins of same-sex anything, Bible-thumping his way into a damn frenzy, warning I'd go to hell if I let their ways divert me from my righteous blah blah blah. I agreed with it all because that was what he wanted me to say. But the worst part was always the same, when he told me it wasn't the sinner's fault—that the devil was in them.

I had this complicated relationship with faith—I wasn't sure I believed anything anymore. Because if any of it was true, then surely there was a reason I was made the way I was? Wasn't it his fault for what I wanted and couldn't stop thinking about when the lights were off and I was alone with myself? Dad would say it's temptation. A test. Something evil was hiding in the corners of my soul. But if it was wicked, why did it feel like the only genuine part of me? Why did it feel like the truth?

I didn't know what to believe anymore—and I was tired of trying to reconcile the different versions of me I saw in the mirror.

"I have a sister." The paperwork showed a genetic

match between Cole Harrington II and this girl I'd never heard of, and it blew my fucking mind.

Dad was all smoke and mirrors on camera, a polished salesman for salvation who made a brand out of faith. He preached love and purity to millions while shaming anyone who didn't fit into his neat little narrative. I always thought he at least believed in Mom, that he was faithful to her until she died. That illusion—that maybe one thing about him was real—was the last thread I'd clung to. It turned out that even that was a lie.

I wondered if Rebecca ever shortened her name to Becca or Becky? I wondered if her mom was kind.

I hoped she'd been happier than me.

I smoothed gel in my hair to give it that tidy, but tousled, magic, then blew myself a kiss. Fuck my head. I was Cole Harrington the damn Third, and I was somebody.

I *am* somebody.

Somebody with a sister and a whole new set of issues with my parents.

I headed out to the next Railers happy-clappy shit I had to go to, but the closer my custom-made Lamborghini got, the more I tensed. Not only was there a guard at the gate who checked my ID before letting me in, but this place was bigger than the place I lived in. Shinier. New money, not old, stunning with glass floor-to-ceiling windows, views over Harrisburg Lake, and an expansive front yard with a ridiculous fountain. Who the fuck on the team owned this?

I parked beside a sweet lava-orange Porsche 911 Turbo S; it was a beast. Zero to sixty in two-point-six seconds, top-tier German engineering, sleek as hell—but my Lambo had it beat. Two-point-four seconds flat, more torque, more raw edge. The Porsche was nice, but mine? Mine turned heads, made hearts race.

Made me think I was something special.

Made the sacrifices worth it.

I followed the noise into the backyard, and the first thing that hit me was the heat and the high-pitched squeals of sugar-fueled kids in the pool. It was big, shaded by strategically planted trees as if someone had curated the scene for a lifestyle magazine. A pool house sat at the edge with one glass wall folded open like some modern art installation.

People were everywhere—too many. Players I vaguely recognized from previous painful social things or awkward preseason meetings. Wives and girlfriends clustered in small groups, fawning over their guys like they were gods, probably laughing at every dumb joke. And so many kids. Running, splashing, crying, laughing. It was chaos.

And none of it made sense to me.

What the hell am I doing here?

"Trick!" I whirled to face my nemesis, Noah Gunnerson, as he stalked over to me. He was constantly pulling me into group chats, always smiling, nodding along to everyone with his stupid head of blond curls. He was dragging someone along with him. "Welcome to our home!"

Oh. Okay then. This was Noah and Brody Vance's place—of course it was. Noah, who was always so freaking nice, even when I didn't deserve it. Even after what had happened after the last game we'd met at when I'd cut him dead. What he could never know was that my dad had been watching that game, eyes glued to every second, searching for ways I might fail his version of righteousness. If I'd spoken to a queer man on camera, even just nodded, he would've cornered me afterward with a lecture on sin and appearances, about how standing next to *"people like that"* was enough to taint me. He would say I was slipping, that the devil was working through me, using kindness and tolerance as bait. And I never argued. For too long, I believed I was wrong. It didn't matter how many times I ignored Noah, or how much of an asshole I was on ice, he stayed calm. Relentlessly, stupidly, ridiculously nice.

We could possibly be friends if things were different and I wasn't so messed up.

"Gunny," I said, gripping his hand firmly, maybe a little too tightly, like I was trying to prove something. Then, I shook Brody's—cool, measured, trying not to let on that I was impressed, overwhelmed by the chaos and the house and the genuine smiles I was getting from people who had no reason to be kind to the new guy after what they'd read about me and my family. The hatred that had been spewed, aimed at some of the people here—they had to be talking about it. About me.

"Drinks over there, food in an hour, barbecue, hope that's okay. Swimming there," Gunny snickered as he pointed at the pool full of kids and leaned into Brody, who held him close and kissed his cheek. "Kinda obvious, right?"

"Just a bit, babe." Brody laughed. "Nice to meet you, Trick," he added to me. "Noah's told me a lot about you."

"Cool." I gave my standard reply. "Bathroom?"

Noah blinked at me—that was not how social interaction worked, and I knew that, but I was tired already. Then, he grinned. "There and there, and also inside by the kitchen."

"Cool." Then, I walked away purposefully and hid in the kitchen with my phone, finding the quietest corner I could. The house smelled like money—clean citrus and polished brass candlesticks or whatever rich racers hoarded. I leaned against the marble island, phone in hand, pretending to scroll.

People laughed in the next room. Kids squealed outside. The muffled splash of water and someone's deep belly laugh filtered through the open doors. I didn't belong here. Not with the happy families and the picture-perfect power couple hosting it all. Not with the team, who'd probably already written me off as the arrogant asshole from Atlanta before we even touched the ice as a team. If only they knew how much of an act I had to put on just to make it through five minutes, let alone an entire event like this.

I hated how small I felt, tucked in this oversized kitchen as if I was dodging eye contact in a school cafeteria, and I couldn't fake the smile.

"Trick? A word."

My stomach fell as Layton Foxx found me. Of course he'd be here, and when I turned to face him, a bright-eyed grinning football superstar stood next to him. Of course, he'd brought Tom with him.

Tom looked ridiculous. Gorgeous, yes—obscenely so. Fitted jeans clung to his thick thighs, and he wore a BoltFuel shirt stretched tight across his chest like he was personally trying to sell product with those damn shoulders. He was taking marketing way too far, but apparently, being unfairly beautiful was part of his charm. My breath caught for half a second, just enough to piss me off because Harrington men couldn't be queer. *It's not right. It's not right.* They didn't like other men in that way. They didn't want dark, desperate kisses or the weight of another man pinning them to the bed, because that went against the word of God.

I clenched my jaw and forced my gaze away, but the image of Tom stayed sharp behind my eyes.

Wrong. Wrong. Wrong.

"It's my day off," I said, raising the beer I'd found but hadn't drunk.

"This way," Layton ordered, and while Tom scampered after him—as much as a six-foot-something, wall-of-muscle football player could scamper—I followed more sedately and attempted to stop the panic rising in my chest.

Layton gestured us into an office lined with photos of motorsport glory days—clearly Brody's domain, a shrine to his speed-fueled career, a place to retreat from Noah's relentless golden retriever energy. But tucked between the F1 action shots and framed champagne-soaked podium wins, I spotted a few hockey pics. A few Railers moments, a youth league trophy, and one of Noah mid-celebration at some youth hockey game.

"It's my day off," I repeated.

Layton held up his phone. "You're not answering my calls, and if you did, then you'd know that Brody Vance is one of BoltFuel's investors; there are people booked to take shots of you and Tom in an informal setting, aka a team barbecue, aka today."

Figures. "On our day off?" I asked, incredulous.

"I'm happy to get it done," Tom said.

"Can we have the room a moment?" Layton asked, and I realized he was asking Tom.

Tom glanced at me with concern, as if he were unsure if I was about to get benched, fired, or eaten alive, and then, he backed out of the office without a word.

Which left me and Layton alone.

What did I do now?

"Do you know who I'm married to?" Layton asked without preamble, arms crossed, brow raised.

I searched my brain. Adler Lockhart. Former pro hockey player. Defenseman. Intimidating as hell on the ice. Queer. "Lockhart."

Layton nodded. "He's the most annoying, exasperating, opinionated, bull-headed idiot I've ever met. Still is. But I love him. He's my forever. My always. No one gets to tell me I can't love him because he can be an idiot. After all, I do—completely."

I blinked, unsure where this was going. "Um, okay."

"Ignore that last bit." Layton sighed, then leaned against the edge of the desk and pinned me with a stare. "Look, even at his absolute worst, Adler was never as difficult to manage as you. This party is for you to get to know the team, but you're coming over as rude and dismissive with a massive fucking chip on your shoulder. Hell, you want people to believe you're an asshole. Congrats, it's working."

"Layton—"

"That's Mr. Foxx to you, kid," Layton snapped. "Now, I've handled egos, Trick. I've managed chaos. And I've never seen someone work so hard to make themselves unlovable."

Ouch.

"You're part of a team now, Trick. That means showing up, even when you don't feel like it. You signed the contract—my contract—which gives me every right to drag your sulking ass into the spotlight until people stop seeing you as a liability and start seeing you as a human being."

"Wait a minute—"

"So, you will go out there, and you will stand beside Tom with your camera-ready smile. You will play nice with him and pretend being here isn't the worst thing in your universe. You will push BoltFuel like it's the nectar of the gods. And you will start acting like someone the Railers family can rely on. Or so help me, Trick, I swear, I will have you smiling next to a schnauzer wearing a team jersey and selling organic gourmet dog biscuits. Don't test me." His rant ended abruptly as he opened the door. "By the pool house."

I opened my mouth to snap back, defend myself, say something cutting or clever or anything at all—but then, I saw his expression. Not angry. Not even disappointed. Just tired. Done. And suddenly, all the heat behind my ribs twisted into a knot I couldn't untangle. I shut my mouth. I was too angry, too bruised, too goddamn raw to form words that didn't sound like another excuse.

"On it, Mr. Foxx," I said instead with sugar-coated sarcasm, then left before he exploded again.

I headed toward the pool house where Tom was already waiting, lounging as if it was another Sunday afternoon instead of a PR stunt. A waiting assistant handed me a BoltFuel T-shirt, and I stared at it for a beat too long before slipping it over my head in the slowest way possible. Stretch. Tug. Adjust. I didn't mean to flex, but old habits die hard—and when I caught Tom watching me with wide eyes, something twisted in my chest. It was a flare of heat; a rush I hated recognizing. His gaze lingered a second too long, and instead of turning away, I shifted slightly, letting the shirt pull tighter across my shoulders. Not because I cared—except I did. I liked the way he looked at me. I hated that I liked it. But I didn't stop.

"You okay?" he asked, voice soft, as if he cared.

I didn't answer. I turned my head and walked past him as if he hadn't spoken.

We did the shoots. The first few were stiff, standard poses in front of the pool, holding the product, some fake smiles that probably looked like grimaces. Brody joined us for some, and his movie-star confidence made the whole thing feel like a luxury brand campaign.

Tom stood beside me and acted as if we were best friends, grinning like this was his year's highlight. I stood there faking it, back-to-back with a man who radiated warmth and ease. He was relaxed, his body brushing mine occasionally as if he didn't even notice. But I noticed— every single time. It sent a jolt through me, electric and unwelcome, heating my skin where we touched. It wasn't only the contact. It was awareness. My jaw tightened, and my shoulders stiffened as if I could block it out. I hated how keyed in I was to every casual graze, every shift that brought him closer. It shouldn't have meant anything. But it did.

I felt his heat, and the clean and citrusy scent of his skin, like sunshine. Beyond us, I heard the thrum of the party, laughter, splashing, and kids and grown-ups blending into a summer soundtrack.

But all I could focus on was Tom. His presence, his quiet steadiness, his stupidly perfect smile. It made no sense that he kept drawing my attention without trying. I didn't want to notice how he laughed, his body leaning just slightly toward mine, or how everything about him felt solid and warm. But I did. And it pissed me off—because I couldn't figure out why I gave a damn.

FOUR

Tom

WHILE I WAS SIPPING FRUIT PUNCH FROM A PAPER CUP, MY attention stayed on Trick as he prowled the periphery of the party like a wary jungle cat. He never seemed to really interact with anyone, even his teammates, which I found perplexing. Yeah, it had to be tough to be jerked from one city to another. I got that. Sports. It happened all the time.

I'd been lucky enough to have spent my entire professional career in Philly. It was home. My dad, stepmom, and three stepbrothers lived in Manayunk. I'd moved from Fishtown at the age of ten when my mother died and spent years ten through eighteen with them in a small, chaotic, trendy rowhome, riding bikes along hilly streets and playing football every damn second of every damn day. The city was my heart, as were the fans who called it home. So yes, I was lucky I'd played in one city for eleven years. I would hate to uproot at my age.

Still, Trick seemed to be distancing himself on purpose. And what a pity that was because he looked so damn lonely. So, doing what I always did when I saw someone who needed something—typical older sibling—I grabbed Trick a cup of sickeningly sweet punch, then ambled over. He saw me coming, those dark brown eyes flaring, then narrowing, as I approached, holding a cup out as a peace offering.

"You looked thirsty," I opened with, placing the cup into his chest, then holding it there until he reluctantly took it. "Cheers."

I slammed mine down. He took a sip, grimaced, then dumped the sugary drink into a nearby azalea. "Yeah, it's for the kids. Didn't know if you drank or not. So, you look like a man who needs—"

He held up a hand. "You have no clue what I need so don't even try to guess. Not that I'd expect a football player to be able to make a calculated prediction."

"A round of putt-putt golf," I finished after the snark he used as a shield—or a weapon if one had thin skin—bounced off my hide. Not that I didn't feel mean words, I did, everyone does, but after spending my life charging through walls of massive men who weren't exactly quoting love sonnets at you when you met head on, most taunts ricocheted away like an arrow off an iron chest plate. And yes, I had been called the F-word a few times, and they didn't even know that I was, in fact, gay as a lark. Would it hurt more if they did know? I had no idea. Someday soon I'd find out, I was sure.

Trick blinked up at me, empty cup in hand. "Sorry. What did you just say?"

Four kids raced by, trampling through the flowerbed with wet feet. I gave them pats on the head as they thundered past, shouting and dripping water from soaking swimsuits. The smell of chlorine and the scent of peachy sunblock made me think of my brothers and the days we had spent in the city pool playing Marco Polo with the other inner-city hooligans we called buddies.

"Putt-putt golf." I stepped closer, then rested my backside on the trunk of an old maple, one sandaled foot on the manicured lawn the other resting on the tree. "I grew up with three younger brothers."

"Congratulations."

I snickered. "Thanks. Joey, Steve, and Larry. Joey is twenty-five and has a nursing job at Holy Mercy Hospital in King of Prussia. Stevie is twenty-three and in the army as a wheeled vehicle mechanic, stationed in Hawaii—the lucky shit. Larry is twenty-two and heading into his senior year at Bucknell on a baseball scholarship. He's got one hell of an arm on him. His idol is Steve Carlton. You know who that is right? Won four Cy Young awards."

Trick seemed confused. "Why are you here talking to me about all of this?"

"Because you look like you need a round of putt-putt. When Larry was little, whenever he would get overwhelmed, I would take him to a local putt-putt. When we were done, he was always lighter. So, yeah, want to play some golf?"

He now appeared to be utterly insulted. Was there something bad about playing putt-putt golf on a warm summer night?

"You honestly think I have nothing better to do than trudge around a stupid, rundown miniature golf course on a Saturday night?"

I shrugged and fell back on a sure tactic. "If you've

never played before, I'll let you win. I always used to let Larry win—just to boost his ego, you know. You know what having siblings is like? Wait, do you have siblings?"

He leveled a glance at me that would have killed a lesser man. "It's none of your business whether I have siblings," he snapped, although there was something in his expression that confused me —almost as if he was angry at that fact. "And I don't *need* you to let me win a damn thing." His growly voice was sexy.

"Ok. I'm just here until tomorrow, then I have to drive back to Philly. We're in training camp now." He was more than a bit miffed. I could see it in the way he held his jaw. "It's okay. I get it. I mean we all know that football players are much better at games of finesse than hockey players. I understand that you're scared."

If looks could kill, I'd have been six feet under. "That is utter bullshit."

"Prove it, Trick." I smiled, then winked.

A splash and a yelp filled the humid air as he chewed on his lip.

"Where is the nearest putt-fucking-putt golf course?" he snarled.

I lifted a shoulder. "Not my town, remember?"

"Fucker." He yanked his cell from his front pocket with so much venom it caught on a string and ripped a small rend. He mumbled under his breath as he did a quick Google search. Then, he rammed his phone so close to my face it bounced off my nose. "Here. Jonestown Road."

"Oh cool." I hurried to remember the address before he stalked off after whipping the empty paper cup at me. I chuckled softly, picked it up, and jogged around the mansion to catch him peeling out in his fancy Lambo. I kicked myself for not driving one of my Italian cars instead of being practical by driving here in my BMW EV. It was fine. I'd catch up in time and then, we would spend an hour together. Maybe he would talk to me about what he was so damned angry about. It had always worked for Larry when he was eight.

NOT TO BLOW MY OWN HORN, BUT IT WAS NICE TO BE recognized.

Gary, the owner of Gary's Goofy Golf, was about to close down when we pulled up. He had no clue who the dude in the Lambo was, but he knew me. Even though the middle-aged man in a Captain Hook outfit was a little pushy, I gave him my best public handshake. After I asked if we could lure him into staying open for us for just another hour, Gary was thrilled to do so. I signed his shirt, a cap for his kid, and took a selfie beside the big sign with a smiling octopus holding a golf club. I also passed him a few hundred dollar bills for staying late for us.

Trick, throughout all of this was, by the looks of him, this close to popping off. When I finally broke free, I hustled over to him, gave him a grin, and told him to grab a putter from the bin.

"He had no clue who I was," he said as he removed a purple putter, then headed out to the course. I grabbed a yellow putter and followed, enjoying the atmosphere of the mini-golf course with its bright lights, happy music, and festive nine-hole tropical pirate design.

"Well to be fair, I've been in the public spotlight for longer than you," I said as I came up to stand beside him on the first hole. "You're what? About twenty-three or four?"

"Twenty-five. And you're what? About fifty?" he asked, then sauntered over to the tee to try his best to get a golf ball through a loop-de-loop and into the cup. A plywood pirate cutout stood over to the left of the first hole.

"Somedays I feel it," I replied and got a crinkled nose in reply. He seemed not to quite know how to handle someone who was not going to rise to his bait. I suspected most took immediate offense to his whole aura. It could be prickly. But as a fan of horned melon, I was more than happy to deal with his pokey exterior. "But I'm actually thirty-three."

He threw me a glance over his shoulder as he took his stance in front of the ball. "No shit. You look pretty good for such an old man."

"Yeah, I work out," I parried. He snorted, then took his shot. The ball rolled halfway around the loop then came back to him. "Oh damn, not enough vinegar. Try putting harder."

"I think I figured that out already all by myself."

I motioned for him to go again, then placed my putter on my shoulder. The theme song from *Pirates of the Caribbean* flowed around us, as did a few hundred mosquitoes. The lights were thick with moths. If the wind moved right, the aroma of the deep fried food tickled my nose. Just how I remembered from back in the day.

"That counts as a stroke," I mentioned casually as the

sound of a car horn interrupted the tunes piping in overhead. The stink eye I got was amusing, and I sniggered softly.

"That was the warm-up," he argued as he lowered his head. His stance was dreadful. Not that I was Tiger Woods or anything, but it was pretty obvious the guy had never held a putter in his life. "This is the first official shot."

"Sure, okay, we'll cheat," I teased. He shot me a middle finger. The man was amazingly easy to distract. That surely couldn't be a good thing for him on the ice. "Since I'm feeling generous, and you're cute, I'll give you a free stroke." His head whipped in my direction, dark eyes round as dinner plates. It took me a second to realize what I'd said. "Oh man that sounded dirty. You know what I meant."

"Fuck," he muttered, then putted. This time, the ball did make it through the loop. He hooted with glee as his shot rolled close to the cup. His smugness was comical. With a swagger he strutted to his ball, gave it a tap, and sank it. Then, all full of himself, he turned to look at me. "Beat that, Gramps."

Using my putter as a cane, I shuffled to the first tee, coughing and sputtering like an old man. Trick smiled a wee bit before his amusement faded. I lined up, got comfy, and sent my ball through the loop-de-loop and into the cup.

"Hole in one," I informed him as I returned to old man shuffle to fetch my ball.

"Asshole," he said under his breath before moving to the second hole. Whistling as I tossed my ball into the air and caught it, Trick cemented my assumption about his lack of golfing skills. On the fourth hole, a tricky one where you had to sink the ball into the open mouth of the Kraken, I finally had to speak up.

"Okay, so you're having so much trouble because you're going at this like it's a slap shot contest. You're not Happy Gilmore. Here." I came up behind him. He watched me warily. "I'm just going to show you the proper putting form." With that I took his hips in my hands and turned him towards the ball resting on the tee. "You comfortable with a man pressing up tight to you from behind?"

"Yeah, that's fine." He glanced back for a hot, short second. Something in his gaze made my blood feel fizzy like the punch we'd had at the party. "If you tell me to address the ball I will elbow you," he growled.

"Nope, not today. Next time. What you need to do is get your body and feet aligned parallel to the ball." I came in close to his back, then used my foot to tap his sneakers a little wider apart. "Good, now loosen your grip." I linked my arms around him. "Hold the putter with your left index finger resting over your right pinkie. Now, focus on a smooth stroke, little wrist movement, and keeping a square alignment."

He was a solid man, lean and muscled, tall and firm. Hard planes, long legs. He locked into my arms perfectly like a puzzle piece. He was stiff though. And I could only assume he was not into me being so intimate. I went to move away.

"Guide me through a stroke," he said, the timbre of his voice lower.

"Sure, yeah." I did as asked, guiding him through the putt, his body tight to mine. He smelled rich. Like the finest cologne money could buy. A rich combo of cedar, myrrh, and leather. I let it tickle my nose and fill my lungs as his putt rolled perfectly between two thick plywood tentacles into the monster's beaklike mouth. "Nice. Really nice."

He threw a half smile at me over a shoulder. Wow. Just… wow. That real smile made him even that much handsomer. I could seriously get lost in his dark gaze, so I gave him a clap on the shoulder, then moved away—quickly—before my dick decided to get any perkier. While he might be okay with a dude showing him a golf stance, he was probably not down with a boner in his ass.

Trick stared down at his feet for a second, then quietly stepped aside to let me putt. My game went downhill after that sultry little hug and putt on hole four. I couldn't get rid of the memory of his body tight to mine no matter how I tried. I managed to tie him after nine. But by the skin of my teeth.

"Ahoy mateys! Gary's Goofy Golf Galley is still open if you'd like some root beer and a platter of barnacle fries after your game!" Gary announced as we pushed through the door leading out of the golf course.

I shot Trick a questioning look.

"I could use a root beer," he said, his tone reserved.

So, we followed Gary—who had acquired a fake peg leg during our game—to a small café with one long bar. The soundtrack for *Pirates of Penzance* was now playing as we climbed up onto stools that resembled barrels. Felt like sitting on a barrel too.

Trick threw a glance my way after Gary arrived with our root beers, fries, and yet another thank you for his signed hat. Seemed his son had Downs and loved the Pumas. Since there was no pro team in Harrisburg, Gary explained, it was either root for Pittsburgh or Philadelphia. I jokingly—mostly—said that he had chosen wisely. Gary nearly wept as he shakily wrote his address on a nautical napkin. Then, I told him to look for some season tickets in the mail for him and his boy. When Gary moved away to make a call, I felt Trick's stare burning a hole in the side of my head.

"You want to say something?" I asked, turning my barrel stool to the left to face him.

He frowned at his bottle of root beer before speaking. "You're unreal. Do you naturally come by this All-American Goody Two-Shoes shtick, or do you have to work at it?"

"It's not that hard to be kind, Trick. And as for Gary and his son... my stepmother has a brother who has Downs. It's one of the charities that I donate to and volunteer for the most because I know just how hard it is for parents and loved ones to find the resources they need. I can afford to be generous now."

He stared at me as if I were speaking some long-dead language. "Why now?"

"Why can I afford to be generous now?" He nodded, his right index finger moving in circles over the lip of his bottle as he studied me intently. "Because I make a stupid amount of money. I don't have a wife or kids, just a dog, and so I like to help. I grew up without much. Mom was a clerk at a law office. Then, she died, and I went to live with my father. Four boys in a middle class rowhouse. Dad and his wife both worked hard to keep us fed and clothed, but it was tight at times. So, when I got my first contract, I vowed I'd give back. What charities do you support?"

"I um… I do a lot with dogs."

"Yeah, you and I are blessed. We make more money than most people can ever dream of making, so handing it to those in need just feels good. You know."

"Course, yeah, I know."

But as he lingered in silence over his pop, I had to wonder if he really *did* know. And if he didn't, then what kind of upbringing did he have if he was lacking in such a basic thing as empathy and graciousness. He intrigued me. I needed to know more, peel back a few of his layers to see what I could find.

"So, since we tied, no clear victor was determined," I said and got a curious look from him. "Which is better football players or hockey players. I'm not sure I can go on without knowing, so if you're feeling it, why not drive out to Philly for a few days? Team practice is open to the public. You can see me be amazing, then we can go do another nine holes."

He pursed his lips. Fighting back a smile of sorts before he stared me right in the eye.

"Sure, I can do that. Give me your phone." I did. He filled in his number and then, passed it back. "Thanks for being mediocre."

He rose and walked off, leaving me laughing so hard I nearly fell off my barrel.

FIVE

Trick

It started like it always did—with the sound of a lock sliding into place. Cold metal. My stomach flipped, and I was sweating, though the room was freezing. Flashes came next: white walls, rows of chairs, the clink of a belt buckle. Words on repeat. Perversion. Broken. Wrong. I didn't mean to be bad. I just was. That's what they said. That's what they made me say. They wanted me to pray harder, cry harder, be better. Fix it. Cleanse it. Scream it out. Someone gripped my shoulders too tightly. My knees hurt. My throat was raw. I said things I didn't believe and heard voices telling me I was loved. That love would save me. If only I repented hard enough. The Devil is in you. The Devil is in you.

I looked to one side and there was someone there, reaching a hand out... a sister... Rebecca. Why was she in this room with me? I'm her big brother; I won't let them hurt her.

She looked like Dad, but she was crying, and Dad never cried. She pointed at the mirror. My reflection was all Dad. Lips thin, eyes stormy with religious fervor. A stranger.

You need to leave.

You need to go.

And then, silence. Except for the locked door.

I woke with a start, tangled in the sheets and completely disoriented. My heart thudded as if I'd sprinted a mile, breath shallow as I stared at the ceiling, trying to remember what day it was, what city, what life I was living. The dream was already fading, but my head hurt. My mouth was dry. And all I felt was this itch, this need to do something, say something, fix something. Why was Rebecca in my dreams?

I'd read the file before going to sleep, photos, evidence, a timeline, sworn statements from her mom, proof of a payoff and regular monthly payments. Added to that, the fact that my father was involving lawyers? Yeah, there was no doubt she was my dad's daughter.

But did that make her my sister in anything but blood.

If I have a sister, maybe I wouldn't feel so lonely.

So fucked up and sad.

I grabbed my phone before my brain caught up. The phone felt like it weighed twenty pounds, but I took it off do-not-disturb and called anyway. Rebecca answered on the third ring, her voice cautious, as if she didn't quite believe the caller ID.

"Hello?"

"It's me. Trick. Cole. Your... yeah."

"Hey, Trick," she said, in a quiet voice—a lot less confident than she'd been when she'd come to the practice rink. There was something grounding about hearing her call me Trick. Not Cole. Trick. She wasn't reaching for the name wrapped in legacy and expectation, but for the one *I'd* chosen—the one I felt like I could breathe in. It was such a small thing, but it mattered.

"Hey," I said. My voice was tight, but it didn't crack. Progress. Or maybe denial with good PR.

Another pause. Then, she finally asked, "You called me?"

"Yeah, I did. Sorry, I just… do you want to meet?"

"I'd love to," she said, "as long as you're not bringing a lawyer or CH2."

"No, just me, coffee? Somewhere quiet. Discreet."

"'Discreet'?" She huffed out a humorless laugh. "Hell, we're going to the most out-of-the-way coffee shop I know, where there's no chance of running into anyone who watches Pastor Cole's Sunday morning fire-and-brimstone hour."

That stung more than I wanted to admit. I'd expected some bitterness, but not that kind of burn. Her words hit like a slap—sharp, personal, and layered with years of resentment I hadn't earned, but somehow inherited. "He's your father, too," I said lamely. However, I wouldn't wish him on my worst enemy.

"Yeah? No," she deadpanned.

"I have this thing in Philly, so… can we maybe meet *next* weekend? Sunday morning?" The irony of meeting the product of my father's out-of-marriage fornication on a Sunday morning didn't escape me.

"Sure."

"Can you text me the address of this out of the way place you know?"

My phone pinged with a message. "Done. Eleven o'clock. Don't flake on me, big brother."

She hung up before I could say anything else.

I stared at the phone, the quiet ringing in my ears giving way to a hollow ache. Big brother?

What the hell was I doing? She was just a name on a report, a sudden reality I hadn't asked for. A sister. Rebecca. My DNA was walking around in someone else, and I hadn't known.

I didn't hate the idea of her—I didn't even know her enough for that. It was more like… I didn't want another connection laced with expectations and rules.

And now I was fucked-up. And tired. And I didn't know what the hell I was doing. There was a twist in my chest that wouldn't go away—part anger at my father for the years of judgment and fire-and-brimstone bullshit, part guilt about Rebecca and how reluctant I was to speak to her, and a healthy dose of self-loathing for the shit I'd said to Tom about dogs.

IT ALL CHURNED INSIDE ME LIKE ACID, AND NOT EVEN later, heading to practice and sinking into the leather seats of my Lambo did I actually relax. The usual comfort—the smell of the interior, the engine's purr, the luxury of control—none of it touched the ache beneath my skin. And now I had to drag this mess of a brain to practice and pretend I cared about line drills and camaraderie. I was so tired of pretending. Tired of carrying all this.

I had more messages, but this time from Tom.

I reread the text timestamped at one-thirty in the morning—did football players not sleep?

> Idiot Ball Chaser: Hey, it's me
>
> Idiot Ball Chaser: Tom
>
> Idiot Ball Chaser: The one who kicked your ass
>
> Idiot Ball Chaser: LOL
>
> Idiot Ball Chaser: I meant to say that if you want to cross-promo for your dog charity, one of my buddies on the team works with Fetchadelphia in downtown Philly, so a link-up could be cool. [paw emoji]

Cool? Who even used the word cool unironically or adds paw emojis? And who the hell named a dog charity Fetchadelphia, although I could admit, grudgingly, it was clever. I could lie and tell him that I'd donated, then send an anonymous donation to make it the truth, but it didn't sit right with me, and yeah, it was Tom's fault that I was sitting there, pre-practice, researching dog shelters in freaking Harrisburg.

"Does anyone know any dog shelters?" I blurted out, and the locker room quieted. I waited for someone to say something, but they all stared at me. Yeah, I didn't talk to them much outside of skating with them, but it was an easy question, for fuck's sake.

"CrossRoads," Noah piped up. "My dad played with Max Van Hellren. He used to play for the Railers, and his husband is—"

"Okay." I stared down at my screen to stop Noah

talking—Van Hellren was an old-school D-man. I heard a hiss to my left and some muttering to my right, and I glanced up to find everyone still staring at me.

"What?" I snapped, and no one had the guts to talk to me; they all turned away. Fuck em. I returned to checking into this CrossRoads place as the team headed to the ice. I had five minutes yet, and I wasn't going out to shoot the shit with a team I wasn't planning to stay with for long, but then, someone tapped my skate with their stick. I cursed at the interruption, ready with my best snarl. I glanced up, seeing Cap staring down at me with Carts and Frosty, the team's two As flanking him, and I tensed. Jack O'Leary was borderline furious, his blue eyes cold and hard, and I was confused.

"You wanna explain being rude to the rookie," he said, his voice measured. He'd been grumpy all week, something about his wife cheating on him, and I knew it wouldn't be too long until I got it in the neck from him for something. Yesterday, it had been Petrov, who'd left his socks out. And yeah, that was pretty shit, but there was no need to throw Petrov's lucky socks into the garbage.

"'Rude'?"

"You cut him off."

"I got the information I needed." The truth was, I didn't know how to hold a real conversation, particularly with someone who was looking to shout at me. At least, not the kind where people looked at you and expected words that mattered. Every time I tried, it felt like my mouth was wired wrong, like I was translating from a language I'd never really learned. It was easier to sound like a prick than to risk sounding lost. Maybe I should ask him about his probably-soon-to-be-ex-wife.

Probably not.

"That's not the point," Carts muttered, shaking his head.

"I just needed a dog charity," I said, trying to keep my voice level, although a headache banded my head and made me want to sit somewhere dark and close my eyes tight.

"You've been here all summer, and in pre-season three weeks," Cap says, ignoring my response. "Three weeks of you sitting alone, not talking to anyone except to criticize their play. Three weeks of you shutting down every attempt at friendship—"

"I don't criticize," I defended, "I'm trying to help."

Cap's face darkened, and I knew I'd pushed it too far. How did I fuck up this time? "The Railers traded you for your hockey IQ, not your attitude," he snapped, voice low enough that it wouldn't carry beyond our little huddle. There it was again, Cap's flash of anger.

I deserve that anger.

I felt my jaw clench. I knew I was fucking up.

Frosty sighed, running a hand through his hair. "Look, man, we get it. Trades suck. But we're your team now, whether you like it or not."

"And Noah's a good kid," Cap adds. "You don't have to be best friends with everyone, but basic respect isn't optional.

I panicked, feeling closed-in. and cornered. "I'll apologize."

Cap shook his head. "It's not just about apologizing. It's about making an effort."

"Cap—"

"And maybe start with not being a closed-off asshole for five consecutive minutes. Baby steps."

I was about to snap when I caught myself. These guys were our team's leaders, and I was fucking up. I respected their play, and the way they led by example. Also, there was something in how they looked at me—not with hatred like back in Atlanta, but with exhaustion. As though I was a problem they were trying to solve, not an enemy they were trying to fight. I was so used to that look. Disappointment.

I swallowed hard, and for a moment, I considered telling them everything. The last time I'd felt this unsteady was staring at the DNA report, realizing I had a sister I never knew existed. But vulnerability wasn't my strong suit.

"I'm sorry. I'll talk to Noah," I said, shoving my phone into my pocket.

"Good. Be better, okay?"

They headed out, leaving me with my thoughts and the lingering smell of gear. I stowed my phone and headed to the ice, tracking down Noah and tapping his shin.

"Sorry about before. The CrossRoads thing… that's helpful."

Noah looked at me with surprise, his stick pausing mid-tap against the ice. The wariness in his eyes made me feel like even more of an asshole.

"Uh, yeah. No problem." His voice was guarded, and fuck, I wasn't good at this.

"Your dad knows the guy who runs it?" I asked, attempting something resembling a normal conversation. I could talk to Noah. He was queer, but he wasn't going to make me do anything; he wasn't going to drag me out of the closet screaming; he wasn't going to make my dad try to change me like he'd done before.

Noah's expression softened slightly. "Yeah. Max married Ben and... you don't need to know that... CrossRoads takes in all kinds of dogs—rescues, strays, and owner surrenders. Ben's a dog whisperer."

I nodded, searching for something else to say. "Cool." There's that fucking word again. I sounded like Tom.

We skated a few strides in awkward silence before I added, "I might check it out." See? I could do normal conversation.

Noah's face lit up as if I'd told him he'd made the first line. "Seriously? That's awesome. They're always looking for volunteers. I could, uh, put in a good word if you want. On Sundays, you can walk dogs for a couple of hours."

"I don't need a good word," I said too quickly, my defenses snapping back up like a reflex. I didn't want anyone else interfering in what I wanted to do. This was for me. Noah's smile faltered, and I mentally kicked myself. "But thanks," I add, trying to salvage this conversational disaster.

Practice started before I could dig myself any deeper, and I threw myself into drills with more intensity than usual. I understood hockey. Hockey has rules, patterns, and consequences that made sense. People, not so much.

The coach blew his whistle, and we broke into line rushes. I hung back, waiting for my turn, watching as the first line seamlessly connected on a tic-tac-toe play that ended with a one-timer into the top corner. They celebrated with fist bumps and quick pats on the back, and I felt something twist in my chest that I refused to call envy. I took the puck and drove straight to the net when it was my turn. Noah was open on my right, but I saw a gap between the goalie's pads, and I went for it myself. I scored, but Coach's whistle blasted immediately.

"Trick," he called out, and I skated over, grabbing an energy drink, still high from beating Whitmore in the net. "You had Noah wide open for a tap-in."

"But I scored?"

"That's not the fu—point. You have an issue with Noah?"

"No."

"Then why freeze him out on a perfect pass opportunity?"

I sipped my drink, trying to buy time. The truth was, I didn't have a good answer. I'd spent the years with Atlanta being the primary scorer on my line, and old habits die hard.

"Wasn't thinking," I mumbled finally. "Just saw the opening."

Coach stared at me, and I could tell he wasn't buying it. "Hockey's a team sport, Trick. If you want to be a one-person show, go play tennis."

He skated away, leaving me to stew in my guilt. I knew I was being prickly, but I'd built this wall between me and everyone else so long ago that I didn't remember how to take it down. I rejoined the drill, and when it was my turn again, I fed Noah for the one-timer. The kid buried it, and his genuine smile made me uncomfortable.

After practice, I sat in my car scrolling through CrossRoads' website. Pictures of dogs with sad eyes and hopeful expressions stared back at me from my phone. I paused on a mutt with one eye, and an ear flopped over, something in its expression reminding me of myself—wary, a little beat-up, but confronting the world.

I switched over to my messages and stared at Tom's text. Fetchadelphia. What a stupid name.

Then, I typed in the address for CrossRoads and headed out. I'd donate, get a photo with a dog or two, and then, I wouldn't be lying to Tom.

The GPS led me to a large place about twenty minutes outside Harrisburg. The parking lot was half-full, and I heard barking as soon as I stepped out of my car. A sign with *CrossRoads Animal Sanctuary* was over at the entrance, with a smaller sign beneath it that read *All Walks Welcome*.

I hesitated at the door, suddenly questioning what I was doing there. I tithed fifty percent of my income to the Temple of the Radiant Truth, I could have just told Tom that, and he'd have understood. I didn't know if he knew who my dad was, but my money helped charities.

A woman with gray-streaked hair opened the door before I could knock. "Can I help you?" Her eyes widened slightly. "Oh! You're with the Railers, aren't you?"

"Yeah," I sad, shifting uncomfortably. "I, uh, wanted to donate."

The woman's smile widened. "That's wonderful! I'm Margie, the volunteer coordinator. Come on in."

She held the door open, and I stepped into organized chaos. The reception area was bright and clean, but a cacophony of barks came from deeper in the building. A wall of photos showed dogs with their new families, many wearing *I Found My Forever Home* bandanas.

"Ben's in the back with a new rescue," Margie explained, leading me through a hallway. "He'll be thrilled to meet you."

I followed her, hands shoved into my pockets, wondering how quickly I could donate and leave without talking to anyone. We passed several rooms with glass windows where dogs of all sizes lounged on beds or played with toys. None of them seem like the sad, caged animals I'd expected.

"Here we are," Margie said, pushing open a door to a large room with windows overlooking a fenced yard. A man with salt-and-pepper hair knelt on the floor beside the dog from the website—the one with a missing eye.

The man—Ben, I guessed—didn't look up when we entered. "Hey, Marge, can you grab the medicated shampoo from the supply closet? We need to get Wink on a—" He stopped mid-sentence when he saw me, and his eyes widened in recognition. "Cole Harrington," Ben said, and stood, shaking my hand.

"Trick," I corrected.

"How can I help?"

The one-eyed dog plopped his butt between us and wagged his tail, staring up at me.

"I, uh, came to donate." I reached for my wallet, but the dog whined and nudged my leg with his nose. I froze, unsure what to do with the animal directly in contact with my designer jeans.

"Wink, back up," Ben said gently, and the dog retreated a step but kept his good eye fixed on me. "He likes you."

"I'm not a dog person," I replied, reaching down to scratch behind Wink's floppy ear. I felt kind of pleased when the scrappy mutt threw me a doggy grin and wagged his tail.

Ben just smiled knowingly. "Funny, because he seems to think you are."

I cleared my throat and pulled out my card. "So, how much would help? Five hundred? A thousand? Ten thousand? Can I get some photos for my socials, with um… with Wink?" What would pull at the heartstrings more than a one-eyed dog? That would prove I was a good guy to Tom. Not that I cared what Tom thought. Much.

Ben looked at me curiously. "Any amount helps, but what brought you here specifically?"

"Noah recommended you," I said, not mentioning Tom or my lie.

Ben grinned. "Stan and Erik's boy? I'll have to thank him." He clipped a leash to Wink's collar. "How about Wink and I give you a tour and get you some photo ops?"

I glanced at my watch. "Sure, but I don't have long." Another lie. What would I do, go home and sit in my empty place?

"Won't take long," Ben said, unworried.

I took a selfie with Wink—kneeling beside him with his one eye staring trustingly at the camera—and uploaded it before leaving the parking lot. I tagged CrossRoads, added a link to their donation page, and wrote some bullshit about *"making new friends"* I was sure Layton Foxx would be proud of.

I hesitated before messaging Tom. What was I trying to prove, exactly? That I wasn't a complete asshole? That I did *"do a lot with dogs"*? I stared at my phone, thumb hovering over the keyboard.

Fuck it.

Me: Check my Insta

I tossed my phone onto the passenger seat and started the car. When I returned to my apartment, my post had thousands of likes, and my DMs were flooded with people asking how they could help Wink specifically. A couple even asked about adopting him. I knew Ben would ensure Wink went to a safe place, but what if me sharing the photo meant I inadvertently put Wink on a trajectory to a bad home? Fuck, now I was second-guessing everything.

My phone rang. Dad. That was quick.

I stared at the screen, hoping maybe I'd imagined it, but no—Cole Harrington II, shining beacon of American televangelism, wanted a word. I took a deep breath and answered.

"You spent money on a dog?" His voice was sharp, the kind that drilled into you and found whatever soft spots were left. "A dog, Cole? When there are a million God-fearing parishioners who need help? Who need salvation and guidance? And you're out there funding mongrels?" I didn't argue, I simply listened, and he didn't stop. "You think this is how you serve God? By posing with some one-eyed mutt like you're a saint. You're wasting your name. Wasting the resources God blessed you with."

The guilt hit hard—it always did—like a weight dropped straight into my chest. My tongue felt like sandpaper, and my throat was tight.

"Dad—"

"I don't want excuses, Cole. I want obedience. Stewardship. Responsibility."

Obedience. As if I were a dog myself.

"What happened with the lawyers and that girl who—"

He hung up and I sat there, phone still pressed to my ear, as if maybe the call hadn't ended. But it had, and the guilt and shame were massive. It consumed me. It wasn't just about Wink or the money. It was about everything— about failing to be the version of myself Dad had built in his image. About chasing something real and being told it was wrong. About not knowing if I believed in anything anymore, except that I'd never be enough for him, no matter what I did.

A message from Tom popped up, and I nearly threw my phone out of the window, because if someone was nice to me right now, I'd sit and cry like a fucking baby.

> Idiot Ball Chaser: Dude! That's awesome! That one-eyed guy is a rockstar. Are you adopting him? Do you volunteer there?

And there it was. Another lie I'd backed myself into. I tossed my phone onto the couch and paced around my barren place. The only furniture was what had come with the place. I hadn't done a fucking thing to make a home.

I sat on the couch beside my phone, staring at the

ceiling. What the hell was I supposed to say to Tom now? *Oh yeah, I volunteer at a dog shelter even though I've been in this city less than a month and haven't even unpacked my shit.*

My phone buzzed again.

> Idiot Ball Chaser: Crap, sorry if I'm being nosy. Just cool to see a sports guy doing community stuff that's not just photo ops or throwing money at things.

I sat up. Something about the apology bugged me. As if Tom thought I was this good guy who cared about one-eyed dogs when I was trying to cover my ass for a lie.

And now I was thinking about Wink again.

"Fuck," I muttered, grabbing my phone.

> Me: Not adopting.

> Idiot Ball Chaser: Aww, but Wink wubs you

I had to reread that a few times to make sense of it. Wub... love... what the hell? Wink didn't *love* me; he saw a man who would scratch his ear, that was all.

Whatever Tom said, I wasn't fit to care for a dog.

SIX

Tom

EMERGING FROM THE TUNNEL FOR OUR FIRST PRESEASON home game was always a gas.

Today even more so because somewhere in the stands Trick was chilling incognito. And didn't I find that too fucking funny? Smiling to myself as the team headed past fans being held back with fencing but still reaching out for high fives, I stopped to give a small boy of about six a high five. That was when his father—or I assumed the man to be, as he was holding the boy's slim shoulders protectively —told me to kick those fairies from Baltimore's asses. I got a nudge from another player jogging out behind me. Shocked and sad to see someone saying that kind of slur in front of their impressionable child, I followed Tyrese onto the field. We were clad in full gear, not planning on hitting each other too hard. It *was* only preseason.

The sidelines were packed with media, staff, and the coaches. The temperature was a chilly eighty-one degrees, and the humidity was thicker than the fog in Satan's jockstrap. But that was all part of the game. Every damn eye in Philly was here it seemed, right down to some senator and his son who weren't at the top of my donation list. This particular politician was solidly against marriage equality, and if he thought he was going to get me to stand at his side, thumb up and smiling like a moron, he was wrong. I'd sooner dip my nuts into boiling coconut oil.

Which brought me back to that dad and son. That kind of shit perpetuated the myth that gay men were sissies. And that pissed me off to no fucking end. It also added another reason for me coming out. If young kids, fans and players, could see a queer man playing this game hard and with power, that would wash away those stupid stereotypes. Or at least it'd help. Or would it? I did a few stretches—kicking my legs out and then, to the sides to loosen my hips—as I mulled over whether announcing I was gay would really change anything. This was always a damn seesaw of emotions. Come out now. Come out after you retire. Don't come out at all. Fucking A, it was mentally exhausting. I was still chewing on it when the game started. Lyle Grange, the QB for Baltimore, was an old college friend of mine. Nice guy, great arm, graduated a year or two after me so we'd only played together for a year maybe.

"You look like you chewed steel for breakfast," he teased as we gathered for the coin toss.

"I chew steel and spit out bullets," I joked as the ref dug around for his custom flip coin. Seemed everyone was a little sloppy for the first game of the season.

"You take it easy on me, okay," Lyle said as we made our way off the field after Baltimore won the coin toss.

"If you dawdle, you go down," I teased, stuffed my mouthguard in, and went to line up facing my old college chum.

Lyle wasn't scared. This was all mainly for showcasing talents and building team chemistry. No one wanted to hurt their QB before game one. The first audible was easy to read. The offensive line had holes in it resembling Swiss cheese. My job was being as generally disruptive as I could be to the quarterback and the men defending him. The coaching staff was all eyes as we lined up at the scrimmage line. Nose guard lined up at center and the others took places depending on what play we thought Lyle was going to call. Me, I was on the end, in a three-point stance, ignoring the rookie on the other end who was vying for my spot. Let the kid try. My knees might creak, and my back seize on occasion, but this old horse still had some giddy-up in him. Also, Trick was here somewhere, so I had to perform well, or he would never let me live it down.

Lyle was ready for the snap, his quick mind analyzing the defense looking for the blitz he knew I was going to try to hit him with first. As soon as the ball was snapped, I charged into Ryan Pinner, a solid left tackle, who should have zigged instead of zagged. His grapple attempt on me failed, opening up a slot that through which I charged like a raging bull, my sights locked on Lyle. The QB shuffled back to try to scramble, but my arms came around him in a bear hug. I lifted him up, then placed him gently on his back in the turf.

"You're too old to be that fast," Lyle shouted as I jogged backwards while blowing kisses to the stands.

Way up at the top in the nosebleed seats sat a person all alone. Had to be Trick. Who else would perch that high up? Did he think he was Clint Barton or something? I'd have to tease him about that. When the ref came over to admonish me for picking up the quarterback, I nodded along as if I would change one damn thing, but my sight lingered on the dude in the ballcap, and shades humped up like a dog pooping on a thistle. Did he ever not seem like he was ready to rumble?

"Sorry, man, I'll make sure to ask him to lie down himself next time," I told the ref and got a warning about being close to an unsportsmanlike conduct call. I backed away with my lips pressed tightly shut. We stalled the other team in its tracks and jogged off to allow Ty and the offense to take the field. A young woman in a Puma tee handed me a water bottle. Hydration was key. I emptied the bottle, then raised it to the man in the rafters. He raised a hand, but from this distance, I couldn't tell if it was a middle finger. I assumed it was. Chuckling to myself, I strolled over to sit beside the rookie. "Nice try. Remember to read the line. If they back up, it's probably a pass. If they push in, a run. Lyle is sneaky, though, and will audible line shifts so you got to know that quarterback well. Also, start watching musicals."

I got the oddest look from the rookie. That was my sage advice for the youngster for the day. He would either use it or not. I gave the stands one final glance, then settled in to watch my team cream Baltimore. It was nice to grab a win, even if the fans weren't in heavy attendance. Someone real important to me was here, and that was everything.

"YOU KNOW THAT HOCKEY PLAYER YOU'RE DOING THE marketing gig with?" Ty asked, slinging a towel over his shoulder as we walked off the field after the game. Not to brag, but we'd trounced Baltimore. I'd gotten a sack or two, which I was sure impressed my visitor.

"Yeah," I replied.

"What's he like?"

"Kinda closed off," I began, but then realized I was doing him a disservice. "Polite, a bit snarky. I like him."

Ty cocked his head. "You know who his dad is, right?"

I frowned, chewing that over. "Nope." Given he's Cole Harrington the Third, I figured there's a CH2. Was that who Ty meant? The name didn't ring any bells.

Ty lifted an eyebrow. "You ever heard of Pastor Cole? Big down in Georgia, spreading the word of praise and damnation."

I ran the name through my brain. It seemed familiar, something in the background noise of early Sunday mornings. Ty supplied the rest. "Big-time televangelist. Sunday morning fire and brimstone."

"Ohhh," I said slowly, the image coming into focus. "Yeah, I think I caught something like that once while flipping channels."

"Yeah, that's the one. Weird, huh? That his kid ended up in hockey."

Yeah, it was odd now that I thought about it. "Maybe God told him to follow in the footsteps of the holiest of hockey players, Wayne Gretzky."

"Maybe you're an idiot." Ty shouldered me playfully. I shouldered him back. It had been a damn good day.

SEVEN

Trick

IT WAS ONLY A FIFTY-MINUTE FLIGHT FROM HARRISBURG to Philly. With the right car and no cops, I could've driven it in a couple of hours.

But no, we flew. Because tradition. Because of team bonding. Because—fuck me—the noise.

The back of the plane was in chaos. Goalies, man. Fucking loud, unhinged, caffeinated chaos. Sokolov was laughing so hard he snorted, and Whitmore wasn't far behind. Someone was playing music from a Bluetooth speaker. No one had shut it down. I hated all of them equally in that moment.

And then, there was Noah. Of course, Noah.

He was sitting beside me, all elbows and long limbs, practically climbing over me to talk to the goalies across the aisle.

"—and then, Dad caught me with his stick, like full-on hooked me around the waist, and I went down like a sack of crap. Said, 'That's how you finish a check, son.'" Noah grinned.

Sokolov barked a laugh. "Legend."

"Bet he could still lace 'em up," Whitmore added.

"Oh, he *does*," Noah said, still grinning. "Last summer, he joined the vets for a scrimmage. He skated circles around all of them."

Of course he did.

The great Stan Lyamin. Hockey god. Superdad. Because, of course, Noah lucked out with the perfect family. And I didn't resent it—not really—but I envied the hell out of it, and that made my chest tight in a way I couldn't shake. Like something sharp pressing just beneath my ribs, reminding me of what I'd never had.

Noah leaned back into his seat with a satisfied sigh, jostling my shoulder like I wasn't trying to disappear into the fuselage. "Gotta love my papa," he said fondly, and stared out of the window.

I almost commented that he seemed close to his family, but the words stuck in my throat. What would that even mean coming from me? Close wasn't a language I spoke. Not with my father. Not with anyone. So, I stayed quiet, let it hang there, and stared ahead as if I didn't care.

Noah stretched out and stole the armrest between us. "I've been studying Philly tapes all week—Halme and Bannister are solid Ds—fast, aggressive, and smart."

"We're not likely to play them in a pre-season game," I mused.

The point was that pre-season was all about getting a team to gel and playing the new guys; hence, why I was here in this pre-season game against the Philadelphia Forge, because my gelling in our practice runs hadn't exactly happened. I mean, I was passing more; I was learning the Railers' plays; I was working hard, but something… it wasn't right.

"Shame." Noah fake-pouted. "I know I could have beaten both of them."

I didn't doubt it. He had the raw skill, the pedigree, and most of all, he had self-belief. I'd spent so long trying to walk a line—sabotaging myself enough to keep expectations low, but not enough to drag the rest of the team down—that I'd forgotten what kind of player I actually was. I never attempted to tank the Phantoms— hell, we'd made it to the playoffs—but I'd let the off-ice drama speak louder than anything I did with a puck. And eventually, they'd stopped listening altogether.

"You excited for this?" he asked, elbowing me, and fuck, his elbows were sharp. I loved hockey—it was my escape, my everything—and I was excited. Not that I'd admit it.

"Sure," I said.

My cell buzzed with so many messages when we headed to the bus, thankfully only my real phone, because I'd left my Pastor-Cole phone at home for the first time. Why? Because I didn't want to hear his voice. Didn't want the weight of his words poisoning this fresh start. Leaving that phone behind felt like dropping a chain. It was defiance, yeah—but also relief—and I could breathe.

Noah ended up next to me on the bus, too, still chattering about lines and plays as if we hadn't just spent a flight together. I couldn't check my messages, since we were heading straight to the arena, but I finally got a moment to look when we arrived and sat back in my stall.

At least, that way, I could hide the screen. Seeing Tom's name made me buzz with...

Excitement?

Nerves?

> Idiot Ball Chaser: Have you adopted Wink yet?

> Idiot Ball Chaser: Also—good luck with the game.

> Idiot Ball Chaser: One more thing—I'm guessing you're staying behind when the team goes back

> Idiot Ball Chaser: For the final BoltFuel shoot, I mean

> Idiot Ball Chaser: Maybe I could show you around a bit after. Local spots, best food, stuff tourists don't know about. Unless you've got plans. Just say the word.

> Idiot Ball Chaser: Also, weirdest Philly moment for me so far: a guy roller-skating down Broad Street wearing nothing but a Forge cape... I mean... nothing!

> Idiot Ball Chaser: Hockey fans are wild, right?

> Idiot Ball Chaser: Someone tried to sell me a cheesesteak from a cooler in a Target parking lot. Said it was "artisanal." It wasn't.

> Idiot Ball Chaser: And I saw a dog on the subway. Not *with* anyone. Just... commuting. Philly's wild.

> Idiot Ball Chaser: Anyway, if that doesn't convince you to let me show you around, I don't know what will.

I READ IT ALL TWICE, THE CORNER OF MY MOUTH twitching before I caught myself. The part about showing me around? I didn't hate the idea.

Then, I sent him a GIF of a hockey fan painted entirely in Philadelphia Forge colors, belly-flopping into a fountain outside the arena. Philly fans didn't do anything halfway—love, rage, or shirtless chaos. It seemed fitting.

"Okay, heads up."

I turned off my cell and shoved it into my bag, giving my full attention to Coach Morin. He gave us the usual pre-season talk about testing lines, building chemistry, and not worrying too much about the scoreboard. Then, he turned to the lineup.

"First line," Coach Morin called. "Center—Harrington. Gunny, I want to try you on Trick's right wing. Petrov, you've got left."

Noah perked up at that, straightening as if he'd been offered the keys to the kingdom. I didn't react, he simply nodded, but something electric flickered in my chest. First line. Let's see what we do with it. I knew Noah was a center, fourth line last season, but moving him to wing? That would be a challenge. I exchanged glances with him, and he offered a fist, which I bumped. A center trying on my wing.

What could go wrong?

Everything.

Because I was the one holding this line together. Because Noah was trying so damn hard—wide-eyed and eager, skating as if his life depended on it—and that meant the pressure was on me to make it work. To set the tone. To be steady. And I was anything but. Four to one, the Forge had us scrapping for leftovers with only five minutes on the clock. Coach called a time out, and we huddled around him.

Coach barked at us to tighten up, play smart, cut off the angles—same stuff every coach says when you're behind. But when we broke and huddled by the bench, he stepped in front of me and Noah.

"Fix your shit and fucking pass to your wings!" he snapped at me. Short. Sharp. Loud enough for me to hear over the cheers of the home team crowd. Noah and Petrov had grown more irritable with me as the game went on, pushing hard, skating harder, trying to force a spark where we had none. That was on me. I was the veteran here. I was the one who was supposed to pull this line into something that clicked.

I gave a single nod. No more words. Just get on the ice and fix it.

"It's okay," Noah said encouragingly. But it wasn't okay. Gunny could be as nice as possible, and I would still be out there fucking up.

We hit the ice again with four minutes left and a chip on our collective shoulders. The Forge crowd was loud, jeering, and it only made the ice feel tighter beneath my blades. I'd missed a couple of good looks earlier—tried to do it all myself—and now I needed to change that.

Puck drop. I won it clean and kicked it back to Petrov, who sent it across to our defenseman. We cycled fast, tighter this time, and when I got it back, I didn't overthink.

I saw Noah darting down the right boards, fast and hungry, waving once to signal.

I passed.

Not a soft chip, but a clean, confident tape-to-tape.

Noah took it, burned around their left D—Jesus, he was fast—and drew the other defenseman out of position before feathering the puck backward, right into the slot.

Petrov was already there. One-timer. Back of the net.

Goal horn. Our bench exploded.

Noah let out a sharp whoop and turned right into my chest, thumping his gloves against mine. "There it is!"

Petrov skated past us, grinning. "About fucking time!"

I didn't smile, but I nodded. One play. One goal. Maybe we could do this.

We got a few more looks before the final buzzer, but the Forge took it 4–2. Didn't matter. Something had clicked. Not perfect, not polished, but there was hope—at least in me.

Gunny was buzzing, pulling his helmet off as we hit the tunnel. "I know I won't get to stay on your wing," he said, flushed and grinning. "But fuck, that was amazing. Thank you." He clapped my shoulder hard enough to rock me.

He was thanking me. Why?

I grabbed his arm to stop him, made him glance at me.

"No. Thank *you*, for being there, for letting me work through my shit."

His eyes widened slightly, then he nodded, slow and sure. No teasing. No follow-up. Simply respect.

And yeah, that meant something.

EIGHT

Tom
___

IT WAS A BLUSTERY SUNDAY AFTERNOON, AND WE HAD somehow managed to edge out our inner-state rival, Pittsburgh. And I mean *just managed.* We were in second place in our division and our season had been rolling along nicely until today. There were some cracks showing and we were going to need to patch them up as the season progressed or we'd be sitting on the outside looking in and I did *not* want to end my career not making the playoffs. A Super Bowl win would be a great way to say adios. I already had a big gold ring from our win eight years ago but hey, if you're going to dream, dream big. Seemed everyone was mulling over how a team struggling to tread water in the standings had nearly whipped us so badly. I'd seen some things on our line that needed some attention. Guys not focusing. Way too many offsides. I mean, holy shit, my fellow defensive linesmen were bolting forward before the ball was snapped a half dozen times. Thank god for Kirby Holleran, our kicker, or we would have lost.

The locker room was quiet aside from Tucker who was

running his mouth about the atrocity of male cheerleaders. I rolled my eyes as I toweled off until I couldn't take his bullshit another second longer.

"Maybe you should have been paying more attention to the game and less to the fucking cheerleaders," I snapped, and the room went quiet as a tomb. "If your eyes had been on Benny Kingsley and not the guys and girls with pompoms, he wouldn't have snuck around you and run fifty-five yards for a touchdown."

Tucker opened his mouth to reply when Ty stepped in between us, hands up, calm flowing out of him.

"Okay, enough. We all were scattered today. Tomorrow at practice, we regain our focus and work twice as hard. This is our year!"

Everyone shouted along, even me, but I was tangled up in my own shit again. Stupid of me to allow a bigot like Tucker to throw me off-center, but damn it, I was tired of having to step up and shut down the hate. And here I was entertaining shining a huge spotlight on myself and my sexuality. But if I didn't speak my truth, then I was hiding my truth. Ugh. It was too much at times. I was over it for now. I wanted to see Trick and get some balance.

I ran a comb through my freshly showered hair with more vengeance than the knots really required. Trick was meeting me on the field after the game for another round of promo for the BoltFuel people. Since we'd done hockey last time, these shots were football-based. Several of the guys asked me to join them for something to eat and a short run to the city to see a new movie, but I declined. Using the photo shoot as an excuse because I couldn't really say I was meeting a guy, then taking him on a putt-putt golf date. Not that anyone had said the word date. But given how much time I had spent thinking about Trick—as well as how many times I'd spanked my meat thinking about his lips on my dick—my head was definitely thinking date. Although it shouldn't because the guy was probably straight as a ruler, but there was no denying the heart at times.

"You're too old to be this stupid giddy," I told myself in the small mirror in my locker before slamming it shut, then waving adios to the few men lingering in the locker room.

Taking my time, I made my way to the field. There stood Trick, rocking the casual jock vibe for all it was worth. Chino shorts showing off some killer calves, blue waffle tee, and that Railers dusky blue cap. His sight met mine as I strolled to him, stopping here and there to converse with PR people from the drink company. They handed me a T-shirt with the BoltFuel logo on it and asked if I would pull it on over my tank top.

"Sure," I said with a smile, then, because I wanted to test the waters, I padded over to Trick while taking my tank off to bare my chest. His gaze raked over me, and I got my answer. The man was into men. No dude did that long of a checkout unless he enjoyed the male physique. That made my step a little lighter. Tugging the tee over my damp body, I arrived in Trick's gravitational pull and felt the tug immediately.

"What, no stupid greeting?" Trick asked, and I shrugged. His brows knotted. "You okay? You look kind of down."

Down? Nope, that would not do. I had to shake it off. "Hey there Pucky Brewster." I gave him a sassy wink.

"Age yourself why don't you?" he fired back, and I gave him a big happy hug. Just a fast one. A bro hug mostly, but I left it linger a little longer.

He pulled away, brushing himself down, glancing around as if he was worried someone had seen, but I smiled at him. The PR lady arrived, handed him a tee, and then pushed us around the field until we were standing under a goal post. Trick, much to my enjoyment, also donned his BoltFuel tee. The man had abs and then some, although the way he got dressed was weird, as if he was trying to hide what he had. The photographer, a skinny woman with bushy hair and glasses, told us we were far too bulky for her tastes, but went ahead to take a few million shots of Trick and me holding cans of energy drinks. Then, there were some of us snarling at each other. Something he did naturally but I kept giggling and screwing up the supposed rivalry.

"Cut it out, asshole," Trick warned, half-serious, glancing at our PR lady, who looked like she was one awkward pose away from snapping a clipboard in half. Definitely not vibing with my giggles. Pity people couldn't enjoy a day in the sun with a handsome man to flirt with. I personally was having a ball. "She looks ready to rip our balls from our body and punt them through the uprights."

"You used football terms!" I patted his dark head.

He ducked away and threw me a look of dismay. "Stop touching me," he warned, and yep, he was being super serious now.

"Sorry, my bad. I have a lot planned for us today."

Trick sighed as if he carried the weight of the world on his broad shoulders. I clamped down on my giddiness until the shoot was over. As soon as we were cleared, I yelled thanks and goodbye to the BoltFuel folks, then grabbed Trick by the shirt. He balked. I yanked. Hey, I wasn't touching *skin*, so that was okay, right?

"I have a reservation at Calamity Katie's Putt-Putt Golf for us in an hour. Then, we have tickets to the museum of art. After that, we have a reservation for a dinner cruise along the Delaware River for seven. Then, if you're not too tired, I thought we could check out a club that I know of over on Locust Street."

He blinked at me. "I'm here for three days. We don't have to do it all in one afternoon."

"Oh no, I know that. Tomorrow after practice is the tour of Independence Hall, then the Liberty Bell, and then, zoo. The day after that is a day off so we can visit the waterfront."

"Are you always this way?"

"Mostly, yeah. So, let's go. I'll drive. You follow. We'll go to your hotel, let you park, and then, I'll drive us around. Chauffeur Tom at your service."

He huffed as if putout, but when I bowed like a proper chauffeur would, I thought I saw a smile. We split up then, him climbing into his hire car, me into mine. He was staying at the Four Seasons. Very swanky. A valet took his keys after taking a selfie with me. Trick stood to one side, half-shadowed by a pillar, the brim of his cap pulled low, trying not to be noticed. His arms were crossed, his body angled like he was ready to bolt, and he kept adjusting his sunglasses as if they were a shield. There was a stiffness in his stance, a tension that said being here cost him something. Once checked-in, he ran his bag to his room while I waited in the lobby chatting with the reservations clerks who were huge Puma fans. When he returned sans the BoltFuel tee, we thanked the staff and made our way to my truck. Several people spotted me, so we had to take a few to sign autographs and snap more selfies.

"Okay, sorry. That's pretty common, as you know," I said as we climbed into my 4x4 and took off for Cottman Avenue.

"Yep, happens to me all the time back in Harrisburg."

I picked up the sarcasm but let it slide. Something deep down in this beautiful man made him this defensive. And who better than a man who specialized in defense to figure it out? No one, that was who. I changed the subject, and once he relaxed a bit, he began to lose that crusty exterior. I didn't push for anything personal as we played our nine holes. I wanted him to let those walls down a little. So, when he won the game with one fewer strokes than me, I shook his hand and called him the winner. He basked in that until we stood at the bottom of those famous steps outside the art museum.

"Rocky statue," I explained with a wave of my hand to the statue of Rocky Balboa off to our left. "Rocky steps," I added as I motioned to the iconic stone steps. "Yo, Trickster, you think you got the cojones to run this with me?" I asked in my best Stallone imitation.

"God, that was terrible." Trick gagged a little, then took off like a rocket. The shitter. I laughed out loud as I took off to catch him. Never quite did. Guess my extra bulk slowed me down just enough that the hockey player beat me to the top. Winded slightly, and more than a little sweaty, Trick threw his arms into the air, red-faced, triumphant, as if he didn't care who saw him, and he was completely fucking beautiful in his excitement.

"Two wins. Two. Two!" He waved two fingers in my face.

"Yeah, yeah, I know."

"This is good," he said, glancing over as other folks ran up to do their own Rocky celebration. He hid himself then, but there was no way he could hide himself when this was a huge tourist draw. I nodded at the men as I turned Trick around to get a picture of us with the museum behind us.

"I don't want a photo," he said.

"Tough," I teased.

He leaned in close to view the pictures. I thought about dropping my arm around his neck and had an overwhelming urge to kiss him. I didn't of course, because first, I didn't know if he was into man lips on his. And secondly, I was in the closet and this place was packed with people. With a rush of regret, I once again cursed myself for not coming out years ago. I took the photo and showed him, expecting him to demand that I delete it, but instead he went very quiet.

"Trick?" I asked gently.

"Nice photo," he murmured. "Send me that one where you're looking spent and I'm all young and vibrant. I'm totally sharing that one with the hashtag beat the old man." Wait? Was he teasing me?

I yanked his cap off his head, then ran down the stairs with him in hot pursuit. When we arrived at the waterfront,

I was now in possession of a Railers hat. A small token from him to assuage my wounded pride being trashed by a hockey player in two macho events. The young lady seating us didn't look too thrilled to see a couple of jocks in tees and shorts, but she seated us anyway after the chef ran out to pump my hand.

"He's on the board of the local LGBT community center. Good guy. Great cook," I whispered as we made our way to our table on the upper deck of the cruise ship, in a quiet corner, as Trick suggested. We sat, thanked the girl in the sleek gray dress, and sat back. The night was cooling down now that the sun was setting. The wind off the river was refreshing. I removed his cap, then tried to give it to him, but he refused.

"Consolation prize," he said as he scanned the menu. I was too busy watching Trick to read the meal suggestions. There was something about the way he held himself that appealed to me in some deep way. His dark eyes lifted from the menu. "You do a lot of stuff for the queer community?"

And there it was. Shit. I glanced around the deck. We were a little early, so the tables weren't filled yet. Only one couple was seated across the way, and they were too far and too into each other to eavesdrop. Did I dare tell him? If I wanted this to possibly move into something more, then someone would have to confess their secrets. It was a big step.

"Yeah, I do. I'm gay." There. It was out. Now two people knew. Trick nodded as if not surprised by that news. "No one other than my best friend knows though. So, yeah, if you could sit on that, I'd appreciate it."

"Thanks for trusting me." He stared at me long and hard.

"Are you okay with me being gay?"

"Sure. I'm... sure." He stopped for a moment. "Can I..." Again, a pause.

"Trick?"

The waitress set down water and took our order, then he leaned forward. "Can I trust you as well?"

"Of course."

He bit his lip. Eyes downcast, the tension in his shoulders had to hurt. "I'm bi."

Inner Gay Tom did a happy dance. "Bisexual. That's good to know."

"Is it?" He glanced up at me, his eyes bright with emotion, as if he was one step from crying.

"Do you want to talk?"

He looked horrified. "No."

The small candles on the table flickered and danced.

"Your team is pretty inclusive, right?"

"Yeah."

"But you're not out?"

"No, and you're not either?"

"No."

I wanted to say more. Should have actually, but our drinks arrived, and so did a few more diners, and so any personal talk was shelved until after our cruise concluded. The meal was top-notch, the food divine, and the service stellar. After a while—maybe it was the beer—Trick relaxed enough that we talked nonstop about all manner of things ranging from sports to books to dogs—I pushed hard for him to adopt Wink because that dude needed a good home like yesterday—to cars. When the boat moored, we exited with the other passengers, bellies full, and took a stroll along the waterfront. The area was made for nighttime romantic walks. We watched the skyline come to brilliant light and took in the Ben Franklin Bridge as we enjoyed a refreshment at Morgan's Pier. There were performers scattered here and there, some singers, some mimes, and a few who played violin for donations.

The trees were turning color, the leaves rustling in time to the notes of "La Vie en Rose," which made me feel as if we were taking in Paris and not Philly. Overall, it was stupidly romantic, and he was smiling at me, and so I turned to Trick as we drank in the violin music and prayed my romance game was brisk, or whatever the word was the kids were using nowadays.

"Can I kiss you, maybe behind that tree?" I jerked a thumb at a fat maple and held my breath for his reply.

NINE

Trick

I'D BEEN LULLED INTO A FALSE SENSE OF SECURITY THAT maybe Tom could be a friend. I was trying not to think about the press of his shoulder against mine, the way his hand kept brushing mine as if it were accidental. It wasn't. Something snapped—sharp, fast, and violent, and my temper flared so fast and hot I barely knew what I was saying before the words were out.

"Are you out of your fucking tiny mind?" I barked, glancing left and right as if people were listening. I lowered my voice, and he leaned in. "What the hell, Tom? Were you born an idiot, or did you work up to it?"

His face fell, and I hated how good he looked even then. Hurt made him softer, but I wasn't soft. I couldn't afford to be. All signs of him being happy vanished. I'd done that. I'd taken his happiness and twisted it.

"You know what would happen if someone saw us? If someone took a picture?" My voice was a harsh rasp of disbelief. "You think I've got problems now? That I haven't been skating on thin ice since Atlanta dumped me?

This would finish me. And what about your golden-boy rep, and your smiling PR mask? You think the fans will love a queer on their team?"

My chest tightened like a vise, and I couldn't breathe around the crushing pressure of what I'd done. Sweat beaded at my temples and slid down my back in a cold trickle, and my hands shook despite the heat blazing under my skin. My pulse thudded in my ears, and I felt nauseous as the panic wrapped around my lungs and refused to let go. I could've lived with the flirting. I was feeling slightly happy with the banter, the teasing, the warmth between us —so stupidly glad to pretend we were only friends.

But now, this? There was no denying what he wanted. And the moment I let it out—let myself want—everything else would unravel.

I could see it already. The headlines. The whispers. My fucking career in a trash can. My dad… fuck…

"Trick—"

"Don't," I snarled. "Just don't."

I let out a harsh sound between a laugh and a growl. I couldn't afford for anyone to care.

Because if they saw us—if someone had taken a photo, if the wrong person had walked in, if some intern with a long lens had been nearby… fuck.

I saw it in my head, played out in sickening high definition: What did God do wrong?

I could already hear the panel shows. The radio hosts. The jokes. The sneers.

I imagined the faces of the Railers management with their fluffy rainbow-is-good shit. Hell, they'd be okay, but I'd seen the signs at their games, the homophobic crap that followed Noah last season. Christ, what about my family? The media destroying me. Destroying them? I'd lose everything if I gave into what I wanted.

"Weakness gets punished," my father's voice reminded me from somewhere in my memories. I was his golden boy; I was allowed this hockey career as long as I paid. I flinched. My skin crawled.

I ran then, heart pounding, throat closing, every breath a knife. Tom didn't follow me. Maybe he knew I couldn't take it. I found a cab—don't ask me how—and as soon as my hotel room door shut behind me, I broke. My heart ached, and I curled in on myself inside the door, silent sobs racking me until I was shaking.

I wanted what Tom was offering. God, I wanted it. The warmth, the care, the kiss I'd seen in his eyes before I bolted. I wanted that kiss more than anything. But the thought of reaching for it made my stomach turn. I felt sick. My head throbbed as if it was trying to hold back everything I didn't want to feel.

I closed my eyes and shut it all out. The cab. The city. The man with the too-soft eyes and pillowy lips. I wanted his hard body, and to forget everything.

My cell buzzed with a message notification, and I crawled over the thick carpet to retrieve it, terrified I'd mistakenly sent that awful message.

Idiot Ball Chaser: If you want to talk. Private. Gated.

.   .   .

THERE WAS A LINK TO A MAP WITH A DROPPED PIN—somewhere in South Jersey, over the Ben Franklin Bridge, and when I zoomed out, it was tucked into a stretch of woods along a closed road. A place away from cameras. From questions. From anyone who might see me for what I was. Certainly not the dorms where practice camp took place.

I wasn't going. I told myself that at least six times, pacing my hotel room as if the floor was hot. If I didn't go, this would all fade. He'd get over it. I could move on. But if I did go... I could lay it out clearly. Tell him this wasn't happening and that we weren't doing this. Then, I could walk away, head back to Harrisburg, and pretend nothing happened.

So maybe I should go? To talk?

The thought kept twisting tighter, a knot I couldn't loosen. My chest ached with it—like I needed to purge something, or it would eat me alive. And before I could think too hard, I was already in a cab, a generic Philly cap pulled low over my forehead, the driver whispering to someone on Bluetooth as the city slipped away behind us, and the bridge rose ahead.

Sweat pooled under my collar as I paced the sidewalk outside his gate, like some wired-up junkie waiting for the cab to turn and leave. I didn't know what I was going to say. I didn't have a plan. All I had was this burning in my chest, a wildfire of panic and shame and want. Too much want.

TRICK: OUTSIDE.

. . .

IT DIDN'T TAKE LONG FOR THE GATE TO OPEN. HE CAME out in jeans and a worn hoodie, casual as if we weren't standing on a fault line. His expression was cautious, but hopeful.

"Hey," he said. "You okay?"

That question again. That fucking question.

"Do I look okay?" I snapped, taking a step toward him. He froze, reading the fury in my face. "Because I'm not. I haven't been since you started looking at me like I was something you wanted."

He didn't speak. Just waited.

"I can't do this," I hissed. "You don't get it. This thing between us—it's not a flirtation. It's not cute. It's not harmless."

"I didn't say it was harmless," he said softly. "But it's not wrong either."

"Isn't it?" I laughed, the sound bitter. "You think I can just be yours? The NFL, the press, my dad's congregation, the ministry, you think everyone will nod while I let you kiss me in public?"

Tom's jaw flexed, "I'm sorry, I got caught up in—"

"Do you know who my dad is?"

He dipped his gaze. "I didn't until Ty told me, my friend Ty, he says your dad is Pastor Cole?"

"Brimstone and hell for sinners, Tom! This isn't a fucking romance movie. You don't get to make me think you can rescue me. You won't fix my brain with mini-golf and protein shakes and sunshine."

"Trick—"

"No. You don't get to call me that right now." He flinched. Just a little. But I saw it. "I should've walked away the first day I met you." I was breathing hard. My fists were clenched at my sides, and I didn't know if I wanted to hit something or collapse.

He nodded once. Only once. "If that's what you want," he said. No anger. No begging. Simply quiet devastation.

And I hated him for making me feel like the villain in my own story.

I spun around abruptly, determined to leave, but each step grew heavier with doubt. My throat tightened with every stride, a lump forming that I couldn't swallow. My hands trembled at my sides, and the backs of my eyes burned hot. I didn't cry—not ever—but for one terrifying second, I thought I might. I didn't understand the mess in my chest—grief, fury, need. It made no sense. Nothing did. Not the anger, not the way I wanted to run, or the ache that told me to turn back. I didn't know how to feel this, and that scared me more than anything else. My feet faltered because it wasn't only him I was leaving behind. It was everything I wanted but couldn't have. In a whirlwind of emotions, I turned on my heel and headed back to the house, stormed past him, down the short drive, and into his house through the open door, with him trailing closely behind.

"Cole?" His use of my given name grated on me, igniting a firestorm of frustration. It didn't matter that I'd told him not to call me Trick, but Cole wasn't me.

He shut the front door and leaned there, uncertain. I stalked up to him and jabbed him sharply. "My name is Trick!"

He furrowed his brow, confused. "But you just said—"

My hand meant to jab at him again but, instead, curled into the fabric of his shirt as I yanked him toward me. Our lips collided, my anger changing into something else. Something I'd been fighting since I first saw him standing at the practice facility on day one, looking at me as if I was a puzzle he wanted to solve. The clash of teeth and tongue was everything I couldn't articulate with words. My fingers tangled in his hair, pulling him closer as our kiss deepened.

Surprised by my sudden shift, he stiffened momentarily, then hands found my waist. Heat blazed through me, scorching away every doubt. His grip tightened, fingers digging into my hips as if he was afraid I might disappear. I couldn't blame him. Five minutes ago, I'd been walking away. I felt the hard press of the door at my back as he reversed our positions in one fluid motion. The world narrowed to the hot slide of his mouth over mine, the slight rasp of stubble rubbing my chin. I couldn't breathe, didn't want to.

When we finally broke apart, both panting, his eyes were dark and questioning. I could practically hear the thoughts racing through his head—what did this mean? Where were we going? Why now? These were questions I didn't have answers for—not yet.

"Trick," he whispered.

I stepped back, needing space to breathe. "It means nothing. It's just sex!"

His eyes flashed with something like hurt before his face hardened, and he stepped closer, not touching me, but close enough that I could feel heat radiating from his body. "You're scared."

"I'm not scared of anything," I lied, the practiced response automatic.

His laugh was soft, without humor. "That's the biggest lie you've told yet, Trick. You're terrified."

"This means nothing." I shoved him back and turned the tables as he stumbled back into the wall, and it was me running the show, his head thumping into the drywall. I pressed my forearm across his chest, holding him there while I searched his face. I expected anger, maybe even disgust, but what I found was worse—understanding, as if he could see right through me.

"Stop looking at me like that," I growled.

"Like what?" he asked, not fighting my hold.

"Like you know me." I shoved him again, pushed my leg between his thighs, ground against him, and felt a jolt of satisfaction when his hard cock brushed mine and his breath hitched. "You don't know a damn thing about me."

"I know enough," he said, voice rough. His hands came up to grip my hips, not pushing me away, but holding me there.

I kissed him again to shut him up, harder this time, biting his lower lip until he groaned. I didn't want his insights or his compassion. I didn't want gentleness or kind words. I wanted the mindless rush, the physical release to let me forget everything else. His hands slid under my shirt, hot against my skin, and I arched into the touch despite myself.

Just once.

We didn't leave the hall; my need was too urgent. I tore

at his clothes, buttons scattering across the hardwood floor as I ripped his shirt open. His hands were frantic, yanking my jersey over my head and messing up my hair. I didn't care. All I cared about was the feeling of skin on skin, the way his muscles tensed under my fingertips.

He stumbled, his back hitting the stairs as I pushed him down, and we collided in a tangle of limbs and desperate hands. I followed, straddling him on the steps, the edge digging into my knees. The discomfort was nothing compared to the fire burning through my veins. His mouth found my neck, teeth scraping over my pulse point, and I couldn't stop the moan that escaped me.

"I hate you," I gasped, even as my body contradicted every word. "I hate what you do to me."

"Trick, no," he murmured across my skin, his voice rough with desire.

I silenced him with another bruising kiss, and I ground down into his erection, reveling in the groan that rumbled through his chest.

My hands fumbled with his belt, desperate to feel more of him. His fingers were urgent, sliding beneath the waistband of my shorts. When his palm pressed against me, I nearly came undone right there on the stairs.

"Bedroom," he managed between kisses, trying to stand.

"No." I wasn't patient enough for beds and pretenses of romance. I pushed him back down. "Here."

Something flashed in his eyes—surprise, maybe, or recognition that this was about control for me as much as pleasure. He surrendered with a nod, his hands settling on my hips as I took control.

I yanked at his jeans, shoving them down enough to free him. His cock sprang forth, hard and straining against his stomach. I couldn't look, and I lifted my hips, pushing my own shorts down my thighs.

"Wait," he panted, his hand catching my wrist. "Protection—"

"I'm negative, PrEP," I growled, impatient. "You?"

"Yes, but—"

"Then shut up." I spat into my palm, wrapping my hand around both of us. The contact sent electricity sparking up my spine, and his head fell back to the stairs with a thud. His hands gripped my thighs hard enough to bruise, and I welcomed the pain—something real to anchor me as everything else threatened to spin out of control.

"Look at me," he demanded.

"No."

"I don't want it like this," he managed, voice strained. "Not angry."

"Once and done," I growled, squeezing harder, eyes screwed tight.

"Trick—" My name was a plea on his lips, and I silenced him with another brutal kiss. I didn't want to hear whatever he was about to say. I didn't want soft words or feelings complicating what should be simple.

Our bodies moved together in a desperate rhythm, sweat-slicked skin sliding against the rough fabric of the stairs. The angle was awkward and uncomfortable, and there was nothing gentle or tender about it—just need, pure and primal.

His hands moved from my thighs to cup my face, trying to slow the kiss. I bit his lip in response, drawing a growl from deep in his throat. But he wouldn't be deterred, his thumbs stroking my cheekbones with infuriating tenderness even as our bodies collided with bruising force.

"Stop," I hissed into his mouth.

"Stop what?" he asked, his breath hot as sin on my lips.

"Stop making this something it's not."

He laughed, the sound vibrating through his chest and into mine. "You still don't get it, do you? It already *is* something."

I increased my pace, determined to bring us both to the edge before he could say anything else that might crack my carefully constructed walls. His hips bucked up to meet my strokes, his breathing ragged. I could feel the tension building, coiling tight in my gut, my thighs trembling with the effort of maintaining control.

"Fuck! Trick!" When he came, it pushed me over the edge. My body clenched around nothing as I spilled between us, hot and messy across his stomach. I collapsed against him, face buried in his neck, trying to catch my breath as aftershocks rippled through me.

For a moment, there was only the sound of our ragged breathing and the distant tick of a clock somewhere in the house. Reality began seeping back in, cold and unwelcome. What had I done?

I pushed myself up, avoiding his eyes as I fumbled to pull my shorts back up. My knees ached from the hard edges of the stairs, and tomorrow, I'd have bruises to remind me of this moment of weakness.

"Trick," he said softly, reaching for me.

I jerked away, nearly stumbling as I stood. My body

felt as if it didn't belong to me—shaky, raw, burning with a dozen things I couldn't name. I wanted to scream. To cry. To punch something until the pressure cracked my chest open. But nothing made sense. Not the kiss. Not the way his hands had felt on me. Not the terrifying ache twisting through me now, the one that felt too close to grief. I didn't understand what I was feeling—regret? Disgust? Or was it fear? I'd spent years burying this part of myself, and now it was breaking loose, and I had no map to follow. "Don't."

He sat up slowly, wincing as he adjusted his clothing. A red mark bloomed on his neck where my mouth had been. The sight of it sent a confusing mix of pride and shame coursing through me. I pulled out my phone to call a ride share, and he took it from me before I was done.

"Stay."

"No."

"We can talk."

"I'm not fucking talking."

"So that's it?" he asked, still sitting on the stairs, gazing up at me with those eyes that saw too much of me. "We just pretend this never happened?"

"That's exactly what we do." I fingered my disheveled hair, trying to piece myself back together. My fingers shook in the strands, not from exertion but from the coil of emotions wound too tight in my chest. I felt brittle—like one wrong word, one wrong look would tear something open inside me that I wouldn't know how to put back together. I clenched my jaw, blinked fast, and willed everything down. Keep it together. No cracks. Not here. "This was a mistake."

He stood, then, and handed me my phone, movements

deliberate as he zipped his jeans and assessed the damage to his torn shirt. "Come on, Trick—"

"Don't," I snapped, scanning the floor for my jersey. "It's just sex."

"Then why not find some stranger at a bar? Why me?"

The question hit like a body check I hadn't braced for, knocking the air from my lungs. I grabbed my jersey from where it had landed on the floor, yanking it over my head.

"Convenience," I lied, the word bitter on my tongue. "You were here."

His laugh was hollow. "That's bullshit, and you know it."

"Think whatever you want." I moved toward the door, needing to escape before I said something I couldn't take back. His hand caught my wrist, his grip firm but not painful.

"You're running again."

"Let go of me." I twisted my arm, but he held fast.

"We can keep it a secret."

"Don't be so naive." My voice wavered, and I couldn't stop my eyes from darting away. I clenched my jaw tight enough to ache, forcing the rest of the words back down. If he saw the flicker of guilt on my face, he didn't call it out —but I felt it. A rush of heat to my cheeks. A hitch in my chest I couldn't explain.

"Why are you so afraid of this?" His voice had softened, which somehow made it worse. I could handle his anger and frustration, but this gentle persistence threatened to unravel me completely.

"I'm not afraid," I said, the lie so transparent it barely made it past my lips. But even as the words hung between us, my body betrayed me. My throat was tight, my palms clammy, and my chest ached as though I'd been hit in the ribs. I was afraid. Afraid of what I wanted. Afraid of what he made me feel. Afraid that if I let myself stay, I'd never be able to return to pretending I didn't care. And more than anything, I was terrified he'd see all of it—that he'd already seen it—and still want me anyway.

"Then stay."

I stared at the door, my escape just feet away. One quick movement and I could be gone, back to my carefully constructed world where hockey was everything, and feelings were a weakness I couldn't have, where I was Trick on the ice and someone else entirely behind closed doors.

"I can't," I whispered, hating the tremor in my voice.

I left and called a cab as soon as I was far enough away.

TEN

Tom
_____

THERE WAS NO POINT IN REACHING OUT TO TRICK TO TRY
to salvage this night.

I didn't know what I would say to the man to get him
to change his mind. And, as I lay awake in my bed wishing
I had my dog to cuddle with, I realized that even if Trick
had said yes and stayed, our lives would be just as fucked.
Neither of us were out. And sure, we could hide and sneak
and pretend we were only buddies, but was that healthy?

No, it was not. I spun around in my bed—back, front,
side, side—and then, when three a.m. rolled around and
I'd not slept, I went out on the patio in my boxers with a
cup of coffee in my hand and watched the stars. I should
get back to the dorms that I was supposed to be in with the
other single guys, not sitting in my own place because I
thought privacy would be better to talk to Trick.

Practice was going to be total shit today. Maybe I
could skip it somehow. Not. Team practice was mandatory.
Unless I had a medical excuse or someone in my family
had died or something along those lines, I'd get a huge fine

for an unexcused absence. Like up to fifty thousand bucks chonky.

So, I chugged more coffee, showered, and dragged my ass back to the stadium as I ruminated on my future. I was so deep into my thoughts that I bumped into Ty exiting the film room. He gave me one look and drew back as if he'd run into a walking corpse. Which was how I felt inside. Dead. Stupid. Stupid and dead.

"Jesus," he whispered. "You forget to use a comb, or a razor, or change your clothes?"

"Nah, I just…" I glanced up and down the corridor. The sounds of men arriving for a game filled the corridors. Soon, the team would be filing into the mess hall for the pregame meal. "Can we talk privately?"

"Sure, yeah." Ty ducked back into the film room, and I followed him inside, closing the door softly. He sat in a chair, one of about thirty that faced a large screen for viewing game films, eyes heavy with concern, as I began pacing. "What's wrong?"

I paused by the window to stare out at the perfectly manicured lawn. "I met this guy," I opened with and got a tender little "Mm-hmm" from Ty sitting behind me. A little brown bird hopped along in the grass as a bumblebee visited a flowering bush in a sculpted flower bed. "I think I fucked everything up. I mean, I think I did. No, I sort of know I did."

"Okay, so why don't you sit down and tell me the story from the beginning so I can know if you did or did not fuck things up?"

I blew out a breath, then turned to face him. He waved a hand at the seat next to him. I moved to it, sat, and started talking. I told him about the shoots, about the chemistry, about how Trick had some issues, but don't we all, and then, I hit the first hurdle at the dinner cruise.

"I told him I was gay," I whispered as if someone had the room bugged.

Ty blinked.

"No shit." He leaned up to rest his elbows on his bare knees. We were all working shorts and tanks before putting our gear on. "That's pretty big, man. You trust this guy to keep that secret?"

"Yeah, he's got his own reasons for keeping his sexuality close to the vest." Trick might be running scared, but he wouldn't sell me out. If he did, he would crash and burn with me, so no worries there. "And like…" I ran my thumb over the rough, scarred skin of my other thumb as I stared at my hands. Huge mitts. Meaty. Marred with white thin marks from a life spent being active on the field and off. "If I didn't let him know I was into men, we couldn't have progressed past friends." I peeked up. Ty nodded. "I guess, I was kind of hoping to find a person to I dunno, ride a bike with him, y'know, like you and Paula do."

"You hate riding bikes," he reminded me gently.

"Well, yeah, but…" I shrugged.

"I know what you meant. So, this guy was not into being with you?" He reached out to tap my knee when I didn't reply. "That happens, man."

"No, it was… no, he was, I think, but he's got all this baggage. The flirting was really heavy, you know?" I met his gaze. He bobbed his head. "And the night was really good. It all felt right. Then, we took a walk along the waterfront. There was this violinist playing this dumb romantic song and I… I guess I got caught up in the moment and him because I asked for a kiss behind a tree, and he sort of lost his shit."

"Ouch, fuck, sorry, man. That hurts. Been there myself a few times." He gave my knee a thump with the side of his fist.

"Yeah it was ugly. Stupid. It was stupid. I'm stupid. What the fuck was I thinking asking for a kiss in a public area? I mean fuck my dumb-ass brain."

"Nah, hey, don't do that. Do not run yourself down. This guy maybe just did you a favor, right? Shutting any kind of sexual shit down when you're closeted—" I had to look away. Ty heaved a sigh. "Did you two hookup somewhere else?"

"Define hooking up." I peeked at him but saw right off that he was not playing the old President forty-two dodge and weave. "There was no penetration." He rolled his eyes so hard he probably sprained them. "I'm not sure what the definition of hooking up is for straights. I sent him a text; he came to my place; we sort of fell on each other like hungry pumas—"

"Ha, funny," he mumbled, then rolled his hand for me to continue.

"Sorry, I'm exhausted, and you know I start punning it up when I'm tired. So, we made out, jerked off, and then, when I asked him to stay, he bolted. End of story. My head was too noisy to sleep, so I watched the sun rise, moped, bought and ate a dozen donuts, and here we are."

"Tom, man, why always the donuts when you're down?" Ty was into healthy eating, big time.

I lifted a shoulder. "They taste better than carrots."

"Fuck, man, all that sugar is going to let you down when you need energy the most. You got that shiny rookie from Penn State hounding your ass to take your slot, and you eat like shit before a game. What the hell, man?!"

I didn't reply for a moment. Then, when I did, all kinds of honesty fell out of my mouth. What was the point in lying to my best friend?

"Maybe, deep down, I want that shiny-ass rookie to take my slot. Maybe, deep down, I'm tired of hiding who I am from the world. Maybe, deep down, I want to date people that I'm attracted to freely like every other lug nut on this team does. Maybe, deep down, I'm tired of living this fucking lie and just want to be happy and in love." Ty rocked back in his chair as if I'd thumped him on the chin with a fist instead of throwing words at him. "Sorry, that was pretty bitter."

"No, that was honest. And I wish I could say I feel your pain, but I don't, not really. I can empathize about how it all must hurt to feel that you need to hide yourself because of who you find attractive. Seems like we take one step forward, then ten back at times when it comes to acceptance in this country." We both exhaled deeply. What more needed to be said? "You think you might want to consider coming out?" Guess he felt that needed airing out, and rightly so given where my fucking life was right now. "I'm not trying to push you into anything. I get it must be a shitty thing to have to stand in front of the world and say you like dick instead of pussy."

"Let's be blunt okay? Stop dancing around the issue," I teased dryly and got a crooked smile.

"There's no need for flowery words with best friends. I

just wonder if now isn't the time for you to free yourself. You're looking at one more year, right? Then you're retiring. I know that's not set in stone, but you've mentioned it to me and Paula so many times that we figure you're just wishing it into existence. If that's the way you see your life going, then why not spend your final year with the Pumas being you. The *real* you. Not the Tom who takes women out to keep the press off his back, but the Tom who dates men that he likes and tells the bigots to fuck all the way off."

I stared at him as if he had said gay people could do such things. Which, obviously they could, but play football and be queer? It seemed too far from my reach even to entertain such a thing. But yet…

"Maybe," I eventually whispered.

Ty leaned forward to clutch my thigh. Hard. Like so hard I winced. "You come out and I will stand right at your side. So will most of the team, the staff, and the fans. We all love you. The city loves you. It's time for you to love yourself. You know what Mama Ru says." I snorted. Yeah, I knew what RuPaul said. And damn it, but that drag queen was right. "Can I get an amen up in here?"

"Amen," I coughed out as someone thumped on the door.

"You good?" Ty asked as he pushed to his expensive sneakers. I bobbed my head, wiped at the wetness on my lashes, and stood. "Whatever you decide, I'm with you."

I gave him a fast, hard hug, then turned him loose to answer the door. Tucker Jones entered the room, taking up a shit ton of space. Tucker was one of my defensive fellows, a massive man with a bald head who sang gospel music like an angel. Tucker was also more than a little homophobic at the best of times and horribly homophobic at the worst of times. He had learned, through multiple fines and benchings, to watch what came out of his mouth in front of the coaching staff, but when it was only us guys, his disgust leached through.

"Thought maybe you two were late to eat because you were in here fingering each other in the ass," he said jokingly. But there was no humor in the comment, only underlying dislike. "Kidding. You know that. I know you two are normal."

I shot Ty a warning glance, then took a step to close the distance between Tucker Jones and myself. My chest bumped his.

"Nope, I'm saving my fingers all for you, Jones." I held up my beefy middle finger, then flicked his nose with it. That did not go over well. If not for Tyrese sliding between us, a royal rumble would have broken out. What ended it the fastest was the arrival of one of the Puma staffers at the open door. He stuck his head in, eyes wide when he spied two hulks squishing the team's star quarterback between them like Ty was the bologna stuck between two pissed off slabs of white bread.

"Fulkowski, Coach wants to see you after you eat," the staffer called out before dashing off to report back to Coach that me and Jones were flattening Tyrese.

Tucker mumbled something unkind about my mother. Ty gave him a shove toward the door before slamming it in Tucker's scowling face.

Ty turned to look at me, shaking his head while chuckling softly. "You keep that kind of shit up and your streak of winning Mr. Congeniality will come to an end," he said as I took a cleansing breath. "Got to say, that was a nice comeback. That guy is an asshole. If he points at the watermelon at the buffet while looking at me one more time, I am going to cross that table and shove a set of tongs up his racist ass."

"I'll hold him, and you tong him."

We high-fived, then made our way to the meal, my head plugged up solid with thousands of different thoughts and worries about me, Trick, the future, and where Tom Fulkowski was going after this season. I wasn't a terribly religious man, but if ever a soul needed divine intervention, it was me, and that time was right now.

Fortunately for Tucker, he kept his distance. I'd never seen that little exchange before. If I had, I would have jackhammered Tucker Jones into the ground and to hell with team spirit. Bigots. The world would be a much nicer place without all the unfounded hate.

I ate slowly, my appetite low, even though I knew I needed energy to fuel the machine. I picked at my food. The chicken and pasta on my plate sat untouched. The only thing that I dug into was some oatmeal for the comfort food vibe. Mom always made me oatmeal on school mornings. Man alive, what I wouldn't give for a Mom hug right about now. She would know what to do. She always did. Moms had a way of untangling things, be they knotted shoe laces or raveled heart strings. I couldn't stop thinking of Trick. The passion we had shared had been intense, fueled by fear and frustration and lots of want. But I'd been too pushy. I saw that now. I had let my loneliness and affection for the prickly puck pusher override my common sense.

If he ever spoke to me again—big *if*—I needed to move more slowly. Take my time. Let him see that there was a future with me. That I would take care of him.

Someone jostled my chair as they passed. I got an apology from the lanky rookie with the gleam in his eye as he exited the dining hall to suit up. I looked at the guys at my table and excused myself to go talk to Coach. Ty gave me a wan smile that I managed to return before I ambled out into the corridor.

On my way to Coach's office, I passed photos on the walls. Framed jerseys. I paused at the jersey of the most revered Puma of all time. Albert Wright. Quarterback in the early-to-mid sixties. Blond hair, blue eyes, all-American boy out of Wisconsin who rivaled Joe Namath in not only flash and pizzazz, but in passing skills. Albert was Mr. Charisma, who posted a few four-thousand-yard seasons himself. Now he was close to eighty and living in a home as CTE claimed him day by day.

Staring at the dark blue and gold jersey, I asked myself what I wanted my legacy to be when I reached that age. What was I leaving behind for younger players to emulate? Albert had been one of the first white players to demand integrated rooms for all players in the early sixties. Albert had stood up for what was right. He didn't back down or hide from the press or the haters back then. He stood arm in arm with his fellow players. I ran a finger over the glass to trace Albert's iconic number seven before setting off to find Coach.

He was in his office, as always before a game, sipping

some of that green tea that was supposed to do wonders for his digestive tract. Coach McNair was in his late fifties, slim as a beanpole and possessed the wildest red hair I'd ever seen. He kept it tamed with some sort of gel that smelled like mango and banana. He lifted sharp gray eyes from whatever he was doing on his laptop to motion me to enter. I did so, closing the door behind me, and made my way to an office chair that made me worry if it would hold me or not. When I eased into it, the thing groaned in agony.

"You wanted to see me?" I asked as I dropped my elbows to my knees. Both had scars from surgeries, stark white lines against somewhat tanned skin. I'd given more than my heart and soul to this game. I'd given up my body as well.

"I did. Rumor has it that you were seen coming into camp with a dozen donuts in hand." Well fuck. I'd hoped I'd been sneaky enough. Guess it was hard to be covert when you were my size. I didn't think Jerry the security guard had ratted me out, so that meant someone at the dorms or on the ground crew of the complex had run to Coach to snitch. Coach closed his laptop to stare at me with weary resignation. "I know you know the rules about junk food, Tom. And hey, I get it. I love a good jelly-filled as much as the next guy. You're old enough to know how shit works here though. We like to focus on nutrition and performance. Not like this is your first year. God knows you're not a young buck eager to rub the velvet off his horn every night." Coach was a big hunter. What horns had to do with Boston creams I had no clue, but I just nodded along. "No more stops at Prangelli's before a game. I do not need to have to listen to the team nutritionist reading me the riot act over some damned Dutch crullers."

Ugh.

I let my eyes close for a long, long moment. Out of all the infractions I was capable of breaking, sneaking eclairs was pretty low on the list. But this whole donut thing was way deeper than a sweet tooth. I had binged because I was seeking comfort in food instead of looking for the solace my soul needed in the truth. I let it all sink in, the entire last twenty-four hours, and then, I felt a calm settle over me as what Ty had said washed back up like a wave on the shore.

You come out, and I will stand right at your side. So will most of the team, the staff, and the fans. We all love you. The city loves you. It's time for you to love yourself.

Ty was right. How could I ask a man to care for me when I wasn't caring for myself? I couldn't. I'd never be happy, *truly* happy, until I was being me, wholly and honestly.

"I need to tell you something, Coach."

He sighed as he braced himself for what I could only assume he imagined was me telling him I committed murder or held up a bank or was recorded smacking around a hooker.

"I'm gay."

ELEVEN

Trick

_____

BEAN & GONE WAS A CRAMPED LITTLE COFFEE SHOP
tucked between a laundromat and a tattoo parlor, its
windows steamed up from the AC running full bore.
Inside, it was too bright, the overhead bulbs buzzing
faintly, and way too loud, the clang of the espresso
machine competing with indie folk music blaring from
tinny speakers. The air was thick with the bittersweet scent
of burnt coffee and heavy cinnamon, like someone had
scorched a tray of sticky buns and decided it was good
enough to serve. There was one wall of graffiti and boards
with ads for sports teams and study groups, house shares,
and a whole load of second-hand notices for everything
from bikes to bedding—a student hangout and not
something I'd ever experienced. Going straight from draft
to team was what I'd wanted—a way to get out of my
father's control—but how much had I missed out on?
Dorm room pranks, late-night pizza runs, debating life at
three in the morning with roommates who turned into

family. I'd skipped over all of it, charging straight into a world where everything had a price, including friendship.

Although second-hand bedding? Eww.

Or was that my privilege showing?

I picked the table at the back, where no one could sneak up on me, and ordered their strongest black coffee. I didn't need sugar. I didn't need milk. I needed to stay sharp.

Rebecca was already ten minutes late, and every time the door chimed, my stomach twisted. I was ready to decide this whole thing was a mistake and bolt; that maybe the paperwork had been a prank or a scam or some elaborate fucking joke the universe was playing on me.

But then, she walked in, and I saw him in her, the same hair and eyes. A feminine version of me.

She wore jeans, a battered backpack slung over one shoulder, and a navy blue University of Pittsburgh hoodie with a gold *Pitt* logo stretched across the chest. She twisted the fraying strap of her backpack around her fingers, a nervous habit that made her seem even younger and more uncertain. Her hair was pulled back into a messy bun, and she looked cute. She scanned the room until her gaze caught mine, then smiled—a little hesitant—and crossed the floor toward me.

"Hey," she said, casual and light, as if we were old friends catching up after a long day, not two strangers whose entire world had just shifted. Or at least mine had shifted—I had no idea who she was, but she'd known about me for as long as her mom had been gone.

"Rebecca," I said, standing awkwardly. My hand

hovered for a second—handshake? Hug? Run?—before I stuffed it into my pocket.

"Yep. That's me," she said, dropping into the chair across from me and tossing her bag to the floor. She reached for a menu, her hand shaking slightly when she picked it up, and my gut twisted again. Either she was nervous to talk to me… or she was a hell of an actress.

"Sorry I'm late. The bus broke down," she said. "But I figured you might think I was running a con for your money or something and bail, so I sprinted two blocks in these." She lifted a foot to show a pair of busted sneakers. "Dedication, right?"

I huffed to cover the awful feeling in my gut about how many pairs of sneakers I had in storage that I'd never wear. "Depends on what you're dedicated to."

Her smile dimmed slightly, but she didn't flinch. "Not your wallet, if that's what you're thinking." She set the menu down and leaned forward, then headed over to the counter, coming back with coffee, and it seemed as if she'd taken the time to consider what to say next.

"So—"

"Look, I want to get this out first. I don't want your money. I don't want your father's money. I don't want anyone to know I'm anything to do with him. I don't want a freaking kidney, okay? I just… maybe wanted to get to know my brother. If that's something you want, too."

Brother. The word lodged in my throat.

Almost without thinking, I blurted, "You don't want to talk to my—our—father?"

Rebecca recoiled so hard she nearly knocked her

coffee over. "Jesus, no. Fuck, no." She scrubbed a hand over her face, her whole body going stiff. "I don't want anything to do with CH2. I don't even want to breathe the same air after what he did to my mom."

Relief hit me so hard I sagged in my seat, the tension I'd been carrying since she'd walked in loosening a fraction. "Good," I muttered.

She tilted her head, studying me with a skeptical look. "'Good'? Or is that your way of hoarding CH2's money for yourself?"

My stomach twisted. "So, you *do* want money?" It killed me that my father could be right when he'd told me that.

She groaned, rolling her eyes so hard I thought they might pop out. "It was a joke, asshole."

I blinked, caught off guard. "If you need help, I can give you money. Don't ever go to him."

"I don't need money," she said firmly. "Mom's life insurance is covering college." She squared her shoulders like she was daring me to argue.

"Still," I muttered, "if you need—"

"I. Don't. Want. Your. Money." Her voice cracked like a whip, final and fierce.

"Just… stay away from him," I said, voice rough. I stared down into my coffee as if it had answers.

"You getting possessive over there? Don't want to share Daddy?"

I fixed my stare on her. "Fuck no. He's… not someone you want in your life."

"Don't worry," she softened her tone. "I figured that

out a long time ago. He was just a man with ambition and one night, he… they…" Rebecca cleared her throat, clearly overwhelmed. "… it wasn't consensual."

I almost rose out of my chair, ready to hunt down my asshole of a father and demand to know everything, but something kept me sitting, because Rebecca needed me to hear this.

"Fuck," was all I offered.

"And you don't have to believe any of this." She tipped her chin. "I believe what my mom said."

I leaned forward. "I believe her over anything my sperm donor says."

"Really?"

What could I say that wasn't too emotional, or make her think I couldn't handle it? "I know him," I said. And I did know him. He might be all godly righteousness and pretend sunshine, but I'd seen the hate under his skin. The same hate that had sent his sixteen-year-old son to a conversion camp.

"… drove Mom to get an abortion and, when she refused, he had her sign an NDA and paid her money to keep quiet. She took it and ran, and I grew up thinking my dad had died. She only told me when…"

"I'm sorry she's gone." That was important for me to say.

Rebecca sniffed. "Me too." I caught raw grief in her eyes. She smiled, but it wasn't the bright grin from earlier —it was smaller, sadder.

I reached over the table and squeezed her hand. "Genuinely sorry."

"It's just me now, you know." She shrugged, fiddling

with the sleeve of her hoodie. "I'm at Pitt. College is hard enough without feeling like you're the only person on the planet, and I never had a sibling, you know?"

My throat tightened. I nodded, swallowing hard.

"Me neither," I said, voice low.

We sat in silence for a moment. Not awkward. Not angry. Just... quiet.

Then, Rebecca pulled out her phone and navigated to her photos. "Want to see her? My mom, I mean."

I nodded, my heart hammering. Rebecca slid the phone across the table, and I found myself staring at a woman with kind eyes and Rebecca's smile. She was sitting on a park bench, autumn leaves scattered around her feet, caught mid-laugh.

"That was last year," Rebecca said. "Before the cancer got bad."

I studied the photo, wondering if this woman had hated my father as much as I did. If she'd known what he was capable of.

"She looks happy," I said finally, handing the phone back.

"She was. Mostly." Rebecca tucked the phone away. "She never talked about your dad until the end. She told me I'd know his name after she was gone but made me promise not to look for him. When my lawyer explained it was Pastor Cole, with all his shit"—she waved her hand, dismissive—"I found your Instagram after she died. I didn't want anything to do with him... but wanted to know if I had family left."

I shifted in my seat, uncomfortable with the sudden vulnerability between us. "And what did you find?"

"You're a dude with a team that's currently shit, too many cars, and a perfect Instagram life." She smirked. "Though your captions are kind of emo for a pro athlete."

I snorted, nearly choking on my coffee. "Jesus."

"What? It's true. All those sunset pictures with quotes about shadows and light? Very deep, bro."

For the first time since walking into this coffee shop, I laughed. It felt strange, like exercising a muscle I'd forgotten I had.

"So," she continued, leaning back in her chair, "now that we've established I don't want your money and you don't want me talking to our sperm donor of a father, can we maybe just try being siblings? Just... see what happens?"

I gazed at her for what seemed like an eternity. The term *"siblings"* felt right and wrong all at the same time, a bit like coming to terms with my sexuality—an internal tug-of-war between discomfort and acceptance.

What would it be like to have someone in my corner I could talk to?

About Tom?

"If people find out, he'll want to be involved. I'd need to put things in place to protect you from the media and from him," I said finally. What secret was worse? Fucking with Tom on the stairs or hiding a sister?

Rebecca's face softened. "You're worried about protecting me? That's... kind of sweet, in a paranoid sort of way."

"Not paranoid. Practical." I tapped my fingers on the table. "My father has people who watch me, track what I do, who I talk to. If you suddenly start showing up in my life, he'll want to know why."

"We'll be careful," she said with a shrug. "Anyway, you might want to read this." She rifled through her bag and pulled out a worn envelope and handed it to me. I took it as if it was a live grenade—what else could she tell me? "Read it, although long story short, I get a million if I stay away."

I didn't read it; I shoved it back into the envelope and slid it over to her. "Take the money."

"I don't want the money."

"So, wait, you want to contact him instead?" I was so confused.

She leaned over and flicked my forehead. "Duh, the two aren't mutually exclusive. I don't want his money. I don't want to see him." She hesitated, picking at the cardboard sleeve on her cup. "I just want to know you. That's all."

"I've never had anyone," I admitted quietly. "Not really. Not someone who wasn't being paid to be in my life. Teammates, coaches, lawyers, managers. Everyone's got an angle."

Rebecca nodded slowly. "I understand. Look, I'm not asking to be part of your public life. Just... maybe coffee sometimes? Or texts? I don't know." She laughed nervously. "This is weird for me too, you know."

I took a deep breath. "Coffee sometimes could work. Messages, too." I pulled out my phone, hesitating before unlocking it, then waiting for her to give me her number. Instead, she reached for the phone, and I balked. This was my private shit, my messages with Tom, porn links, what if…

"Give me the phone," she murmured, and in the end, I passed it to her. If everything came out? If she knew, what did it matter? After typing in her number, she sent herself a text, then passed it back and replied.

We'd completed the social connection ritual and now… well, it was about coffee, but I felt unsettled and weird.

Rebecca's smile was bright enough to light up the dingy coffee shop. "Tell me something real about you. Something not on Instagram."

I hesitated, running my finger along the rim of my cup. I could say a thousand things—about the team, my apartment, the endless stream of parties and appearances that filled my calendar. But none of that felt real. I could confirm her thoughts about me being gay, but that was nuclear. I could say to her that I met someone who wouldn't leave me alone, but what if I let it slip it was a man? Fuck. There had to be better things I could tell her.

"I think I hate playing hockey," I said quietly.

Rebecca's eyebrows shot up. "Seriously? But you're like… good at it. Really good."

"Thank you."

"I bet you hear it all the time."

"Nah, mostly I hear about my wasted potential." I sighed. "Still, it was the only way out of my parents' house. My father's control." I stared at the scratched tabletop. "Hockey was the one thing I was good at that he couldn't take away. He couldn't play it for me. He couldn't do the drills or take the hits. It was mine."

"And he let you have it because…?"

"Because it made him look good. Pastor's son, NHL draft pick?" I laughed bitterly. "Great PR. Plus, he gets a cut of everything I make."

Rebecca's eyes narrowed. "How much?"

"Doesn't matter." Why did I say anything?

"It does."

"It's a charity thing," I mumbled.

"How much?"

I was angry then. How could she ask that kind of private thing? I stared at her, ready to fight, but her expression was so calm and patient it took the wind out of my sails.

"Fifty percent," I admitted quietly. "It goes to his ministry. Tax write-off for me, free money for him." I didn't mention the secrets he kept as long as I kept paying him.

Rebecca whistled low. "That's fucked-up."

"Yeah. Well." I shrugged, trying to make it seem like it didn't matter. "It's just money, and he leaves me alone for the most part."

"It's not *just* money when it's your life," she said fiercely. "To get away from him, you're doing something you *think* you don't like, and he's still profiting from it? That's…" She trailed off.

"That's my father," I finished for her. "And I do like hockey, I just… I used to love hockey, but now…" I'm fucking it all up.

We sat silently for a moment, the coffee shop noise washing over us. Rebecca was fidgeting with her cup, turning it in circles, her brow furrowed in thought.

"What would you do?" she asked finally. "If you could do anything besides hockey?"

The question caught me off guard. I'd spent so long viewing hockey as my escape route that I'd never considered what came after. What I wanted for myself.

"I don't know," I admitted. "Never thought that far ahead."

"Bullshit," Rebecca said, not unkindly. "Everyone has dreams. Even if they're stupid or impossible. I'm planning to go into teaching, but I love theater, and I'd also like to be an actress, and that's not practical."

I felt a sudden, fierce tug that it was entirely practical for her to do whatever she wanted if she had a big brother supporting her.

I looked at her, this stranger with my eyes, who somehow seemed to see right through me. "If I'd gone to college? Then, architecture," I said finally. "I like buildings. The way they're structured, how they stand up against everything. How they can be beautiful but functional at the same time."

A slow smile spread across Rebecca's face. "That's actually really cool."

"Yeah, well." I shrugged again, uncomfortable with the pride I felt at her approval. "Not exactly compatible with an NHL schedule."

"So what? You're what, twenty-five? Twenty-six?"

"Twenty-four," I corrected.

"Even better. You could still go to school. I mean, not now, obviously, but eventually." She gestured vaguely. "Hockey players retire young, right? And you're on what, ten million a year? I mean that's a lot even if CH2 has half."

"Yeah."

"Tell him you're not sending him money anymore."

"It's not that simple."

"Why?"

"Because he's..." I lowered my voice, leaning in. "He's got dirt on everyone. That's his thing. He collects secrets like trading cards and has a whole deck on me."

Rebecca studied me, her eyes narrowing slightly. "What kind of secrets?"

I felt my pulse quicken recalling the moment he found me, and the consequences, the school, the conversion therapy... the hell. Not to mention my mom and her reputation in shreds. "The kind that would tank my career." I swallowed hard, wondering how much to reveal.

"That sucks."

"Yeah." I traced a coffee ring on the table. "But I've got four, maybe five more years of peak playing time. Then I can figure out what's next. Be myself."

"And in the meantime?" she asked.

"In the meantime, I play. I smile for the cameras. Try not to fuck up and do what I'm told." I paused, staring at my half-empty cup. "Even though it worked, and I got traded out of Atlanta, I try not to think about the fact that I'm miserable most of the time."

"What worked?"

"Huh?"

"You said it worked, and you got traded from Atlanta. What worked?"

Had I really said that out loud? "It's nothing."

"No, it's not nothing." She stared at me with one eyebrow raised.

"I needed to get out of Georgia without blowing everything up with my father. So, I made myself a bad guy and they traded me. A win for me, a loss though, because I was hoping to get a lot further than Pennsylvania."

Rebecca's expression softened, and for a second, I thought she might reach for my hand, but she didn't. Instead, she leaned back in her chair and crossed her arms.

"That's a pretty shitty way to live."

I laughed, the sound hollow even to my own ears. "Yeah, well. Welcome to the family."

"No," she said firmly. "That's *his* way. It doesn't have to be ours."

Ours. The word hung between us, strange and new and somehow comforting.

"He's just as invested in your secret, right? He doesn't want to lose the chance of money, even if he's probably raking it in from the gullible. So maybe you take the money away from him, reveal the real you, he loses all credibility after spouting all the anti-everything, women know their place, God will strike you down crap he comes out with, and you'll be happy."

Happy with someone like Tom who was as much in the closet as I was?

The thought of Tom made my stomach twist with both longing and dread. Could I really just come out? Walk away from hockey? Let my father's precious reputation crumble while I built something real?

I snorted. "Right. Just come out, lose my career, hand the Temple of the Radiant Truth, aka my father, a PR win about how they 'tried to save me,' and watch my entire life implode. Easy."

Rebecca rolled her eyes. "Lose your career? You really think the Railers team gives a shit if you're queer?"

My coffee cup froze halfway to my lips. I hadn't actually said the words out loud. "I didn't say that I was—"

"Please," she waved dismissively. "I'm not stupid. I can read between the lines. Didn't they have that guy, the first out player, like way back?"

"Tennant Rowe."

"Yeah, and then others. Anyway, gay, bi, pan? Who cares? Besides, my roommate is pan. Her parents were super religious too." She leaned forward. "And for what it's worth, she's happier now. Living her truth and all of that."

"I'm guessing your roommate isn't in a sport where guys still throw around homophobic slurs like they're high-fives."

"Fair point." Rebecca stirred her coffee. "Well, whatever you do"—she pointed between us—"you have me as backup."

"'Backup'," I repeated, testing the word. "You barely know me."

"I know enough," she said. "I know you're trapped. I know you're miserable. And I know from my mom that Pastor Cole is a manipulative bastard who doesn't deserve to control either of our lives. It's probably going to be messy as hell." Her voice softened. "But living a lie is killing you, big brother. Isn't it?"

The question hit harder than a body check. I'd spent so

long compartmentalizing, building walls between the different versions of myself, that I hadn't stopped to consider the toll it was taking.

I stared at her, this fierce stranger who shared my blood, a knot of fear, relief, and a tiny, aching flicker of hope twisting deep in my gut. "Yeah," I finally said. "It is."

We chatted a while longer, and then, it was time for her to leave and for me to head home.

"Take this," I handed her one of my credit cards, even though she shoved it back at me. "For emergencies."

She scowled—oh my god, it was like looking in the mirror when I didn't get my way. "Jesus, Cole. I bet it's got like a ten-k limit, and I'm not owing anyone that kind of money."

"Nah, a thousand max," I lied. "I'm covering it; you can call it eighteen years of birthday and Christmas presents. Buy some new sneakers, at least."

"Cole—"

"Trick. Call me Trick." I needed that from her.

"Trick, then, and okay, I'll get the sneakers." I was so damn relieved, and then she sighed heavily. "It'll be nice to have the money to eat again."

I sat upright. "What? The fuck? You don't eat?"

She snorted a laugh. "I'm messing with you."

I stared at her, laughter welling inside me, and I snorted. "You little shit."

She blew me a kiss. "You know it."

I dropped her a short way from her dorm, so in her words, no one thought she had a sugar daddy. I was relieved that today had gone well. We went straight into messaging when I got home—silly stuff about our favorite bands and movies, but halfway through a particularly thorny discussion over *Star Wars* vs. *Star Trek*, a message from Tom popped up, and my heart stopped.

Humiliation at what I'd done washed over me.

Tom: How's it going?

I'd long since changed his name from Idiot Ball Chaser to Tom, I had no idea why. And how was he still talking to me after what I'd done? After losing my shit so badly and fucking around with him on the stairs.

I stared at the message, paralyzed by the emotions it triggered. Shame, want, hope—all of it churning in my gut as if I'd swallowed broken glass.

Me: Fine. You?

The response came immediately, as though he'd been waiting.

Tom: Thinking about you.

The three words hit hard.

Me: Why?

Tom: You know why. We should talk about what happened.

My fingers hovered over the screen. What was there to say? Sorry, I freaked out after we fooled around. Sorry, I'm a closeted mess who can't handle wanting you? Sorry, my father would destroy both our lives if he found out.

> Me: Nothing to talk about. It was a mistake.

> Tom: Was it?

I didn't know how to answer. I stared at my phone, the screen dimming from inactivity before I jabbed at it to keep Tom's message visible. I wanted to see him again just because I wanted to apologize. Was it a mistake? Every logical part of me screamed "yes." My career, my freedom from my father, everything I'd built depended on maintaining the careful façade I'd constructed. But something deeper, something I'd spent years trying to smother, whispered no.

My phone buzzed again.

> Tom: I'm in Harrisburg.

Panic surged through me. *What? Why?*

> Tom: Bye Week.

> Tom: Give me your address.

> Trick: No. Why?

> Tom: We need to talk. Give me your address, or I'll call BoltFuel to get it myself.

> Tom: Don't think I won't hire a PI to find you

What? Was he threatening me? I sent my address before I could think, paranoia riding me hard.

Tom: I'm fifteen out.

I scrambled off the couh, heart hammering, knocking the TV remote onto the floor with a loud clatter. I cursed—fumbling to grab it and toss it onto the coffee table—my hands clumsy with panic. Fifteen minutes. Fifteen fucking minutes to decide whether I was going to let him in or barricade myself behind my door and pretend I wasn't home.

TWELVE

Tom

STANDING OUTSIDE THE DOOR OF TRICK'S PLACE, I WAS suddenly swamped with doubt. Tons of it. I was drowning in uncertainty.

Generally, I wasn't this pushy. And now that I'd sort of strong-armed Trick into speaking to me, I felt like a big, dumb aggressive dickwad, who should have been able to take the brush-off—or more like the slam of the door in the face—and gotten on with my life. I should have taken this time off during my bye week to work on myself more.

Staring at his door as if it held the secrets to the universe instead of a peephole and a mail slot, I considered turning and leaving a dozen times. Maybe sending him a text saying that I'd changed my mind. That he had the right to tell me to stay away.

"Fuck." I sighed, letting my brow drop to his door. It was a good solid door, I was glad to note. No one would break it down without a struggle.

Eyes closed, I felt the door move from my head. With a jerk, my gaze flew from my feet to Trick standing inside the doorjamb, eyes wary, looking at me as if Satan himself had rung his doorbell. He stood there in shorts and a tank showing off his toned biceps. I had caught a glimpse of incredibly muscled calves before I had yanked my gaze from the floor.

"Oh. Hey." I took a step back. He leaned on the door, barring me from entering. "How did you know I was here?"

"The thud of your rock head on the door."

Ah. Yeah, that had hurt. "Right. Well, I drove here to talk to you. All the way here, I was filled with righteous cause."

"Okay." He didn't move. Just held his ground, arms folded over his chest in a defensive manner, as if he thought I might act out. Which, given my fucking bullheaded attitude, was to be expected on his side.

I glanced around. "I know I kind of forced this meeting."

"'Kind of'?"

Ouch. Totally true but, still, ouch. "Okay, more than kind of, and I am sorry for being such a shitty sort of guy."

"You drove here from Philly to tell me that you're a big steaming pile of shit? Dude, you could have saved the gas. I know that already. Is that all you wanted to say?"

"No. I, no…" I took stock of the hallway we stood in, then turned my attention back to Trick, still barring my entry into his space. "Do you want to do this where everyone can hear?"

"I'm not sure that whatever you need to say is possibly personal enough to warrant—"

"I told my head coach that I'm gay." I winced at how

chipper that sounded and dropped my voice. "Which is really kind of exciting but scary all at once."

The sour look of consternation fell from his face. Shock replaced irritation. He blinked a time or two, then opened the door wider. I stepped past him, taking in the rental apartment he called home. Nice place. Basic. He'd not personalized the space any, but it had lots of potential. It was right off the Capital Area Greenbelt, so there were trees to be seen through the windows.

I turned to face him after a moment of crushing silence. He was staring at me as if he had never seen a dopey-ass football player before. I wiped my hands on my shorts, smiled stupidly, and blew out a breath.

"Yeah, so that's what's happening in my life. Got anything cold to drink?" I asked, which got me an exaggerated gape.

"Tom, seriously, did you play football without a helmet as a kid?"

"Nope, always wore head protection."

He shook his head in disbelief. "Then your mother dropped you on your head as a baby. No way did you just say what you said out loud in my damned corridor where all my nosy neighbors could hear without having some head issues. No one announces something that major with all that golden retriever energy. It's just not done. No one is that happy to come the fuck out to their coach."

I crossed my arms over my sweaty Puma tee. It was hot out, and I hated AC blowing in my face, so I'd had the windows down on the ride here.

"First off, *Cole*, I said I wanted to talk about it inside, but you were all Gandalf on the bridge of Khazad-dûm."

His stared at me blankly. "Are you even speaking English?"

"Jesus. Secondly, I think being excited to be able to be myself is something to be happy about. So, if you want to call me a golden retriever guy, then go right ahead. I can think of worse things to be called. Nothing wrong with being loyal and affectionate. Maybe you should throw me a ball?"

"You are unreal."

I shrugged. "Yeah, probably, but it's where I'm at right now. I told my coach, and when I go home, I'm stopping in King of Prussia to tell my folks. I wanted you to know because I like you, a lot, and I wanted to say that I'm willing to do big things to make us work."

His brow furrowed. "Do not tell me that you are coming out for me. Just don't put that on me, Tom."

"No, no, not at all." I saw the fright in his eyes and felt myself drawn to him. I held back but just. Shit, maybe I was a golden guy. I see someone I care about sad and worried, and all I want to do is kiss them and make them smile. This was not a kissing moment, though. "It's been eating at me for years now, to be honest, but I was scared. Ty has been telling me forever to just be honest with the world. Whoever doesn't like me being gay can fuck themselves. Ty is good that way. I would love for you to meet him and his girl, and my family." His eyes flared. "I mean, whenever you're ready. Or maybe you'll never be there, and that's good too."

He looked like a rabbit surrounded by a pack of beagles. But there was only one dog barring his way to his burrow, and it was a goofy golden defensive end. So, I did what I knew he probably wanted me to do. I moved around the room, slowly, and went to his front door. His gaze followed me around the apartment, wary, but also dark with some other emotion that I couldn't read.

"So that's it. I'm going to make my announcement before the first game of the year against Pittsburgh. The Puma organization is scrambling to get me and my speech shined up for the press and fans since it's a Monday night game. My agent is growing a second ulcer as we speak, he informs me."

He stared at me openly, his teeth working his bottom lip. I had to clench my fists to stop myself from padding over to rub my thumb over that full lip to free it from his teeth.

"Why are you making it a big thing?" His words hit me as I placed my hand on the knob. I raised an eyebrow. "Why can't you just be you without fanfare?"

"Trick, I'm not doing this for the fanfare. I'm doing it because I'm tired of living a lie. I should have had the guts to do it back in college, but I held back because I was young and intimidated. I'm sick of being frightened. I want to find a man to date, to love, to spend my life with. I was hoping that man was you, but I'm sensing that you're not into me like that so—"

"God, you are so dense."

"Uhm…" I wasn't sure I wanted this to end on an insult to be honest.

"I am into you like that."

"Oh. Cool."

"Lock the door."

My brain was a little slow on the uptake, but it caught up when Trick removed his tee, exposing all that pale creamy skin pulled tight over a torso thick with muscle. "Lock. The. Door." I fumbled for the deadbolt as he untied the string holding his shorts in place. They slid down over thick thighs to puddle on his bare feet. My gaze moved to his cock and lingered there, enraptured as his prick thickened before my eyes. I glanced up from his cock to find him wearing a look that screamed that behind his bravado was a man terrified of being himself for whatever reason. There were many. I knew that all too well. "If you don't want to do this with me, then whatever…"

Ah there was that practiced nonchalance. "Trick, I *so* want to do this with you." I tugged my T-shirt over my head, pitched it to the left, and didn't even glance at the sound of a lamp thudding to the floor. "Come here."

He faltered for a second, and then he began to move closer, each step erasing a line of tension until his brow was smooth as glass when I gathered him into my arms. I wondered what his famous father would think of his god being the one who created Trick to be a bi man. Nothing good if the snippets I had read online were true. Trick's lips on mine flushed the thoughts of the hateful televangelist away with a warm rush of passion. I snugged him close to me, moving him to the right, as I slid my tongue into his waiting mouth. He sighed into the kiss, letting me take control.

"I love your taste," I groaned when we broke for air, his arms now linked around my waist while I bumbled around, unsure of where to take us other than somewhere vertical. The sofa was right there, but I wanted to lay him down, spread him wide, and feast on him like a buffet. "Bedroom?"

"Mmph, here, fuck me here." His hands skimmed over my chest, then to my hips. With a tug my cock bounced free, the head slick already. He crawled over me like a lemur, mad with desire. "Fuck me here on the floor."

His fingers dug into my short hair as he nipped at my lip. I peeled him off gently, took his wrists in my hands, and tenderly looped them around and behind his back. His nostrils flared as his cock jumped, the twitch felt through my own rigid prick.

"We're not dogs." I ran my teeth down the side of his neck. His head fell to the side. "Well, I guess I am, but you're not. You're special. I want to love you somewhere soft, somewhere you're comfortable, somewhere I can take you apart kiss by kiss, stroke by stroke, and thrust by thrust."

"Yes, yes take me apart," he whimpered.

I released his hands, swept him up with a huff—as damn he was heavy—and carried him down a narrow hall. The bedroom door was open. I strode in, my arms full of writhing hockey player, and laid him out on the wide queen bed. It was unmade and covered with piles of folded wash. Trick pushed the clean clothes to the floor, then reached for me.

"You want me to use a condom?" I enquired as he cupped his balls, then lifted them to show me his hole. I bit down on the inside of my cheek to stop myself from leaping on the man right then. Yes, we had had this talk before, but that was just a hand job. This was going to be me filling his bubble butt with spunk so…

"No, no condom. We're both good. Just get inside me now."

"Pushy puck pusher," I chuckled as I spread his legs wider to accommodate my bulk. Then, because it was so pretty and so damned hard, I dropped a kiss to his navel, then fell on his cock like a starved man. Trick yelped and dug his heels into the bed. I pressed down on his hips, showing him that I was leading this show. He melted into the bedding as I tongued at his slit then swallowed him whole.

"Fuck, fuck, oh fuck, Tom." Hearing my name shouted by this man made my cock pulse in warning. I had to slow this down a bit, or I'd be done before I ever sank into him. His hands found my head. I peeled his fingers from my skull and pinned his wrists to the bed beside his hips. A sound like a man finding Nirvana floated from him. I sucked on his head for ages as he seemed to enjoy that a great deal. "I do want this. I want this… you… I want it so fucking bad. Ah, shit, shit!"

I pulled off with a loud *pop*, worked my way back to his lush lips via his tender little nipples, and kissed him senseless. He was like an eel under me, moving constantly. Sensual to the nth.

"Lube?" I asked after giving his lower lip a tug.

"Nightstand," he panted, his legs now around my waist, his hips rolling like the tide. I sat back on my heels, taking a moment to admire his beauty. It reminded me of being in Florence a few years ago with Ty and Paula. We'd taken a tour to see the sculpture of David on a hot, hot, oh so hot day, and even though hundreds of people were packed into the Accademia Gallery of Florence, I'd felt as if I were there alone as I gazed on male perfection. Now, once again, I was drinking in the beauty of a perfect male form.

"You are the most gorgeous man," I whispered as I coated my fingers with slick.

Trick smiled at me, a genuine sort of dreamy smile I'd not seen before. "I think you're gorgeous too," he confided so quietly I had to strain to hear him.

With a grunt of awkward acceptance of the compliment, I bent down to kiss his belly as I wiggled my fingers under his heavy nuts. Trick threw a leg over my shoulder with a sigh. My fingers slid into heat and tightness. He reached for me. I shook my head. His hands fell to his heaving chest.

"Good man," I praised as my fingers sank in deeper, finding a knot of nerves that sent Trick into a spasm of contracting muscles. "Easy, baby, easy."

"I need to come," he barked, then pouted as I removed my fingers and took my cock in hand. He grabbed his dick. I moved his hand away from his length. "Fucking A, just do me!"

Seeing him so needy for my dick made it weep. I used my thumb to wipe the pre-cum around the swollen head, applied some thick lines of lube, and worked it over my dick while Trick whimpered softly.

Without a word, I tapped my cock against his entrance then pushed in. Easing past that bit of resistance timidly. Trick was having none of that. He arched up and hooked his leg around my back, slamming my cock into him. We both growled in pleasure.

"Fuck me. Fuck me, Tom. Now, hard, wipe away the rest of the world," Trick pleaded.

I began to move. Deep, slow thrusts rocking the bed into the wall, as well as my world. I'd been with other guys, sure, but something about this experience was beyond the others. He clung to me like a limpet when his orgasm crested. I watched him throughout his release and felt the hot wash of spunk between us as he blew apart with only the pressure of my cock on his prostate. Truly the hottest thing ever. I dropped my head, pressed my brow to his, and drove into him relentlessly until my balls contracted. Trick dug his heel into my ass to push me deeper as my cock spurted over and over. Endlessly it seemed. Unable to catch my breath I went to my elbows, pinning Trick tightly under me as my dick kicked. He latched onto my mouth with his, licking deep, tonguing my teeth as his ass clenched around me.

"Holy shit," I gasped across his puffy lips as my dick pulsed a few more times.

"Don't pull out. Please," he whispered breathlessly.

I nodded, kissed his lips once more, and buried my face into his sweaty neck where it joined his shoulder. His fingers moved over my heaving back as we floated downward from the summit, my cock growing flaccid.

"I gotta ease out, baby," I said and got a sleepy sort of grumble in reply. Smiling at the tender sound, I moved reluctantly, cum oozing out of him as I did. I pulled up a corner of the sheet and tucked it between his legs before falling onto my stomach, face in the mattress as the fitted sheet was balled up under Trick's shoulders. Or somewhere. Not really sure. Didn't really care.

Trick lay beside me for a while, quiet, his leg resting over mine. When the silence began to move from sated to awkward, I pushed up to my elbows, ignoring the crick in my back from being in a yoga sphinx pose, and glanced to the side.

Trick was staring at me; his brow still damp with sweat and his lips tender and bright pink. The man was gorgeous. And, amazingly, he wasn't wearing that panicked look.

"Thought maybe you fell asleep," I lied. I'd been worried he'd been tumbling into the pit of shame after making love.

"No, I just kind of spaced out." He moved to his side to stare at me with that piercing look he sometimes had. "You're not like any other guy I've ever met."

"Oh?" I smiled a little, unsure of where this was going. Knowing Trick and his fears, I suspected he was going to dive into a meltdown and throw me out into the hall like a bag of sweaty trash. "Is that good or bad?"

"Not sure." He ran a finger over an old scar on my shoulder. "What's this from?"

"Rotator repair," I answered softly, unwilling to startle him. It reminded me of stumbling upon a fawn in the woods and trying to interact with the timid creature. Trick was a flight risk for sure and, this here, was not a moment I wanted to lose. He was mellow, open, and temporarily willing to let those walls down for me. "First season in the pros. If you go over my body with a magic marker and make an X on every scar I got playing football, I'd look like a well-used tic-tac-toe board."

He smiled knowingly. "We play hard sports."

"Yep." I heaved myself to my side to face him. The air conditioning was on, spreading the smell of sex, sweaty man, and the fragrance of some air freshener thingy somewhere in the room. "It takes its toll. In a way I'm glad this is my last year. I want to settle down. Find a man to cuddle with at night, take to dinners, and generally fuss over."

His gaze moved from the scar on my shoulder to my face. "You want that with me?"

"I do, yes, if you'll have me."

He nodded, lost in thought, then he leaned over to kiss the white scar from my shoulder surgery before rolling from the bed. I watched him moving. Tossing the dirty sheet aside, padding into another room—the main bath, I soon discovered as I heard the sound of a shower being cranked on. I sat up, slowly, unsure if that was my dismissal or if I should join him. I had pushed myself on him more than I should have already. I eased myself to my feet feeling incredibly uncomfortable.

Trick peeked around the doorframe, holding out a massive pink and purple beach towel with a flamingo wearing shades on it.

"This was the biggest towel I could find." He gave it a shake. I stood glued to the spot beside the bed. One of his sleek eyebrows quirked. "So, are you coming in to wash the jizz off or are you going to stand there looking dumb?"

"Oh. Probably going to look dumb for a few more minutes. Trick, are we done here now or are we going to be talking more? I'm not sure where I stand."

"You're standing in my bedroom. And yeah, we'll talk

more, but for now, I just want you close to me for a little while longer."

That I could do.

That I would *love* to do.

The world and its problems could hang on the line to dry just a little longer.

THIRTEEN

Trick

I WAS AWAKE BEFORE TOM, WATCHING HIS CHEST'S SLOW rise and fall as morning light filtered through the blinds. I'd never let anyone stay the night before. It was a rule— get off, get out. But last night, after the shower that had turned into another round against the tile wall, we'd fallen into bed, damp and spent, and I hadn't been able to form the words to make him leave.

I didn't want him to leave.

Now, he was sprawled across my sheets, one arm flung over his head, the other curled around my pillow. Vulnerable. Trusting. It made something twist in my chest.

What would it be like to wake up to this every morning? To open my eyes and see him there, warm and breathing, tangled in my sheets like he belonged? The thought clawed at something inside me I didn't have a name for. Was I so wrong to want this? Was it so bad, the part of me that ached to be with a man, to be wanted and held and seen?

I'd spent so long convincing myself it was. That

wanting another man meant I was broken or deviant. But looking at Tom, peaceful and real in the morning light, I didn't feel broken—I felt human. I felt hope.

Maybe the worst thing wasn't being queer. Maybe the worst thing was pretending not to be. Emotion surged, threatening to break through the fragile dam I'd built inside myself—but I couldn't let that happen. Not here. Not now. I didn't want Tom to wake and see me coming apart, didn't want him to think I was having second thoughts or losing my grip. What would he even see? Shame? Regret? A man unraveling because, for the first time, I was thinking I could be honest enough to want what I wanted? To be who I was?

I slipped out of bed, careful not to wake him, and padded to the kitchen. Coffee was essential before I could process any of this. As the machine gurgled to life, I leaned into the counter, staring blankly at the wall.

I'd let wild, wonderful, sexy Tom in. Not just into my apartment, but into parts of myself I'd kept locked away for years. And it terrified me.

My phone buzzed on the counter—Rebecca—and I smiled at the thought I could talk to her, but as I opened the message, I nearly dropped my phone.

> Rebecca: I got a cease and desist. I thought you should know. The Ministry of Fucked Up, aka CH2 doesn't want me to contact you.

I typed a message, then backspaced, not knowing where to start. In the end, it was easier to talk directly. I waited a few minutes to calm down, then called her.

"Hey, big brother," Rebecca said.

"Hey." I kept my voice low, glancing back toward the bedroom. "You okay?"

"Yeah, just freaked out. I knew he was monitoring you, but this was fast."

I closed my eyes, resting my butt on the kitchen counter. "How did he even know about our meeting?"

"No idea. The letter came yesterday, but I only opened it this morning. Law firm in Atlanta. Very official, very threatening."

My stomach knotted. "What does it say?"

"The usual legal bullshit. That I'm violating a binding agreement, that I'm to cease all contact with you immediately, blah blah blah. There's a reminder about the million dollars and how I forfeit it by contacting you."

"Fuck," I whispered. "I'm sorry, Rebecca."

"Don't be."

"You should take it," I insisted. "A million dollars would set you up for life."

"And bind me to his rules forever? No thanks." Rebecca's voice was firm. "Look, I'm not freaking out about the money. I'm worried about you."

I glanced toward the bedroom again. "Me?"

"Yes, you. If he's watching this closely, what else does he know?"

The question hung in the air, heavy with implication. What if he knew about Tom? About last night? My blood ran cold.

"I can protect myself," I said, not entirely convinced.

"Can you? Because it sounds like he's got you locked in a golden cage—on the surface, everything looks perfect, but inside, it's control and fear and no room to breathe. It sounds like he's convinced you that this is the only life you deserve, and that's not love, Trick. That's a prison."

I swallowed hard. "It's complicated."

"It's abuse," she countered. "Financial. Emotional. Whatever you want to call it."

"Rebecca—"

"No, listen to me, Trick." Rebecca's voice grew more insistent. "This is exactly what he wants. For us to be scared, to stay away from each other. He's counting on your fear. And I want to be your sister. I want to be in your life."

I ran a hand through my hair, glancing anxiously toward the bedroom again. "It's not that simple."

"It never is with abusers," she said quietly. "But you've got options. You've got me. And whoever else is in your corner. That is, if you want me in your life. I get it if you don't want—"

"Of course I want you in my life, I never had a sister, and I... Jesus, Rebecca... I want you in my life."

"This is serious. He's tracking you, monitoring who you talk to. That's not normal." Rebecca's voice had that fierce quality I was starting to recognize—she wasn't backing down. "What happens when he finds out about something bigger than a half-sister?"

She meant me not being fixed as I pretended to be. I rubbed my eyes, the fatigue suddenly bone-deep. "I don't know."

"Do you have a lawyer? A good one, I mean. Not one he picked."

"Yeah, I have my own guy now." After Atlanta, I'd

learned that lesson. "Rebecca, I need you to be careful. If you're not taking his money, and you keep seeing me, he'll ruin you."

"Ruin me, how?" she asked, half amused, half skeptical, clearly unaware of the gravity behind the warning. She hadn't grown up with him—hadn't witnessed the cold precision with which he dismantled lives. To her, he was just a name, a threat on paper. But to me, he was the monster in the dark, the man who wielded power like a scalpel and carved up anyone who dared step out of line. My stomach twisted with memories best left buried, the ones that smelled like antiseptic and sounded like prayers twisted into weapons. My head throbbed as panic bloomed behind my eyes, and I sank into the nearest chair, overwhelmed by the weight of what she didn't yet understand.

I needed to make her see. "Maybe he can't ruin you with money or a career, but he'll try something. Trust me."

Rebecca huffed, "Trick, to him, I'm a nobody. A college student with student loans and a tiny apartment I share with two other people. What could he possibly do to me when I have the ultimate threat hanging over him? One call and his affair is exposed, and even all these years later, I have proof, and it could destroy him. He had my mom tied up in so much litigation, but when I turned eighteen, and when she got ill, he has nothing apart from trying to buy me off."

I gripped the phone tighter. "You don't get it. He'll dig until he finds something, twist it, weaponize it. He'll hurt you, discredit you, make your life unbearable, all to protect the illusion he's built and keep his reputation spotless.

That's all he cares about. And he'll burn anyone who threatens that, no matter who they are."

There was silence on the line for a moment. "Okay, so what do we do?"

"'We'?" I echoed.

"Yes, we. As in, you and me. Siblings. Family. Remember?"

The word *family* hit me like a body check, knocking the breath out of me. It had been a loaded term for so long —code for control, shame, and walking a tightrope to survive. Family had always meant doing what I was told, being who they needed me to be. But now, with Rebecca... it felt different. The idea that family could mean safety, belonging, even love—it was unfamiliar territory. And terrifying. But also, maybe, just maybe, worth stepping into.

"I think," I began, then stopped, trying to form the words. "I think you should block my number, for now at least."

"What? No way—"

"Just hear me out. If he's monitoring my phone records —and I wouldn't put it past him—then your number showing up is a red flag. We need to be smarter than him."

A sound from the bedroom caught my attention. Tom was stirring.

"I have to go," I whispered. "But listen, get a burner phone. Text me from that. We'll figure this out."

"Fine," Rebecca said, although she sounded unhappy about it. "But Trick? Don't let him win. Not this time."

I ended the call and the air in my lungs turned to acid, sharp and searing, each breath harder than the last. My thoughts spun—what if he hired someone? What if he sent someone to follow her, to hurt her, only because she existed? I gripped the edge of the countertop, white-knuckled and trembling, heart hammering out of rhythm. My chest tightened until it felt as if my ribs might crack. I couldn't think. Couldn't move. I was spiraling.

And then—Tom.

His voice, low and steady, sliced through the panic like a lifeline. "Trick. Hey. Look at me. Breathe."

He was there, crouched between my knees before I even realized I'd dropped to the floor. Gloriously rumpled, shirtless, hair sticking up in wild tufts as if he'd fought sleep and lost, he looked like comfort incarnate. His hands were warm on my thighs, grounding me, coaxing me back from the edge. He didn't ask questions. Didn't press. He stayed there, unwavering, eyes locked on mine, repeating for me to breathe, calling me sweetheart, on repeat.

"Talk to me," he murmured, concern etched across his face, when my panic eased.

I nodded quickly. "He'll hurt my sister."

"Who will? Who is threatening your sister? Wait, you have a sister?" Given I'd told him I was an only child, he was right to be confused. I grabbed him and held him close, burying my face in his neck, tears of frustration choking me. "Trick? Do we need to call the cops?"

"No! Yes. Fuck, I don't know."

"Trick?"

"It's complicated. Coffee? Then we can talk?" I still didn't look up at him, didn't want him to move, letting him hold me up as I processed everything.

"We don't need cops?"

"Not at this moment. But… do you know any security companies?" Sudden clarity swamped me. "I have money, I can get someone to follow her, and I'll do that." I fumbled with my phone, but he took it from me.

"Five minutes," he said and tugged me to the bathroom. At first, I held back, and he wrinkled his nose at me. "Shower," he repeated. "Coffee. Hug. Talk."

I followed him to the bathroom, my mind racing. Tom had this way of making complicated things feel simple— just shower, coffee, and to be with me. As if all the barriers I'd built could be washed away with hot water and soap. Then, I could get security fixed.

Then, I could keep Rebecca safe.

Talk to my father.

Promise him anything to stay away from her.

Under the spray, Tom pulled me to him—not sexual, just steady and grounding. His arms wrapped around me with the kind of care I didn't know I'd craved, his hands moving in slow, calming circles across my back. I stood there, every muscle tense, waiting for the urge to pull away. But it didn't come. Instead, I leaned in, resting my forehead on his shoulder, letting myself sink into his warmth. Letting myself be held.

It wasn't about sex. It wasn't about control. It was about letting someone else carry the weight for a second. And in that moment, I allowed it. I let myself feel small, feel safe, feel… cared for. It scared the hell out of me. But I stayed in his arms anyway, because maybe, for once, I didn't have to be the one holding everything together.

The shower was quick. We were silent under the spray as I tried to organize my thoughts. I watched water sluice down his broad back, tracing old scars and the defined muscles that spoke of years of physical punishment disguised as sport.

"So, your sister," he finally said, voice gentle as he handed me a towel when we were done. "The one you didn't have yesterday."

"Half-sister," I mumbled, wrapping the towel around my waist. "Rebecca. I just found out about her recently."

"Tell me about her," he murmured against my temple.

"Her name's Rebecca. Father forced her mom to have nothing to do with him. She's in college. My father... he doesn't want us to have any contact. His lawyers have offered her money to stay away from me, and she's said no, and so they're threatening her and—"

"Slowly, sweetheart," Tom encouraged, his hands stilling briefly before continuing their gentle circles. His voice was low and coaxing, not demanding, as though he already knew what I wanted to say was buried under layers I wasn't ready to peel back. I didn't want to talk about my father—not now—but I had to. I closed my eyes, jaw tight, the words scraping out like they'd been lodged there for years. He was asking because he cared, and that alone almost undid me. "Why would he want to hurt her?"

"Because she's proof he had an affair and isn't the righteous man he pretends to be." I'd moved way past trying to defend him—hell, maybe I never really had. There'd never been loyalty, just silence. A numb detachment so complete I hadn't even realized how deep it went until Rebecca had cracked it open.

"No one can stop you from knowing your sister."

I pulled away from him, went into the small kitchen,

made more coffee, and stayed quiet, the mug warm in my hands as my thoughts tangled and collided. I couldn't stop picturing Rebecca's face, the fierce conviction in her voice, the stubborn way she refused to be afraid. It echoed inside me, louder than I wanted to admit.

But fear clung to me like a second skin. I kept waiting for the other shoe to drop—for the moment he'd tighten his grip and remind me how easily he could rip my world apart. I leaned my hip into the counter, staring at the swirling coffee, willing it to offer answers.

Tom followed me, stood behind me, his hand on my lower back, steadying me. I wanted to be brave like Rebecca, defiant. But I wasn't there yet. Not fully. So, I breathed in steam and caffeine, trying to believe his words. Trying to believe Tom.

"He'll destroy you too."

"I don't have skeletons in my past," Tom said. "I'm the son of heart-of-gold parents who know all my secrets, with siblings who are strong and love me."

"All your secrets?" I said, freaked out.

"All apart from you." He shook his head. "And hell, I'm coming out, so he can't hold that on me."

"No, you don't get it! Do you remember Dyna Bubble Mint?"

Tom's brows lifted. "The rap artist who had her juvie records leaked?"

I nodded, throat tightening. "Dyna was my first real friend after I broke free of Dad. He was adamant I try out for the NHL after conversion therapy, as though it was some reward that he'd given me, and not my hard work and talent that had paid off. I brought her to the draft as a fuck you. An openly queer woman on my arm, proud and loud. And she paid the price for my rebellion."

"What the hell, Trick?" Tom growled. "Conversion therapy?" Fuck, did I actually mean to tell him that? I wish I could rewind. "Trick?"

"It was him," I said, my voice flat, ignoring that question. "He got Dyna's records from before she transitioned, medical stuff, trouble she'd gotten into as a kid trying to find her place. He leaked them. Buried whatever career she had and turned her into a cautionary tale to remind me he was still watching."

Tom's jaw tightened. "You're sure it was him?"

"He told me," I whispered. "He fucking stood there and told me, like he was proud of it. Smiled like it was justice. Like hurting her was the Lord's work. I was so stunned I couldn't even move. I went on and financed the documentary she did, the tell-all—it was my way of trying to fix something, give her a platform again. And thank fuck, she's clawed her way back, but Tom… that was a warning shot. He'll find something. He always does. He'll destroy Rebecca, me, anyone who chips at the image he's built." I was getting stressed again, worked up, and I needed to be at practice in two hours, and I'd be taking so much aggression with me if I went now. "I'll ask the team, about security, someone has to know someone."

"Okay."

Then, I gripped Tom, kissed him hard, deep, and shoved at my clothes until I was naked, leaning over the counter. "I need this," I begged, "fuck me."

"Trick—"

"Now, Tom."

"Fuck, okay! Wait!" He sprinted into the bedroom, came out with the lube, and then, his hands were on my hips in an instant, fingers digging into my skin with the right amount of pressure. I felt the heat of him behind me and closed my eyes. This was what I needed—something primal, something real to drive away the fear.

"You sure?" he asked, his voice rough with desire but still careful, as he bit my neck, then sucked a bruise lower down.

"Yes," I hissed through clenched teeth. "Please."

When he pushed into me, I gasped, gripping the edge of the counter so hard my knuckles went white. The surface was cold against my chest against the fire building inside me. Tom moved with purpose, each thrust driving the panic from my mind until there was only sensation, only us.

"Harder," I demanded, and he complied, one hand sliding up my back to tangle in my hair.

I lost myself to the rhythm, the slap of skin on skin drowning out the echo of my father's threats. Tom pulled my head back by my hair, just enough to make me arch, to change the angle so he hit the spot inside me that made stars burst behind my eyelids.

"Trick," he groaned, his free hand reaching around to stroke me in time with his thrusts. "God, you're beautiful like this."

I couldn't form words, only incoherent sounds of pleasure as the tension built. This was what I needed—to be taken apart, rebuilt, anchored in my body instead of spiraling in my head. Tom knew exactly how to give me that.

When I came, it was like being shattered and made whole at once. Tom followed moments later, his forehead pressed between my shoulder blades, breath hot against my sweat-slick skin.

We stayed like that for a bit, breathing together, until Tom gently pulled away. I winced slightly as he withdrew, the cold counter pressing my chest and an ache in my hips where they'd been pressed into the edge.

"You okay?" Tom asked, his voice soft as he grabbed a washcloth from the kitchen drawer. He ran it under warm water before cleaning me with tender strokes.

"Yeah," I said, straightening slowly. My legs felt like jelly, but my mind was clearer. The panic had receded to a manageable hum. "Thanks. I needed that."

Tom kissed my shoulder. "I know. Come on, let's get you dressed before practice."

I turned to face him, suddenly aware of my vulnerability—not the nakedness, but something deeper. "Tom, if he comes after you—"

"He won't scare me away," Tom said firmly, cupping my face in his hands. "I've dealt with men like him before. Different contexts, same power games."

I leaned into his touch, wanting to believe him. "You don't know what he's capable of."

"Maybe not specifically. But I know enough." His thumbs stroked my cheekbones. "Look at me, Trick. I'm here because I want to be. Not because it's easy or safe."

I eased away, gathering my scattered clothes. The post-sex clarity was fading, reality creeping back in. "My father has ruined people for sport. Journalists, business partners, and athletes who spoke out of turn." I yanked my shirt over my head. "People who thought they were untouchable."

Tom leaned against the counter, watching me dress. "And you think I'm what? Naive?"

"I think you don't understand what you're getting into. This isn't just about me anymore. It's about Rebecca; it's about you." I zipped up my jeans with more force than necessary. "It's about anyone who stands too close to me when he decides to take aim."

Tom crossed his arms over his chest, still gloriously naked and somehow managing to look composed despite it. "You think I walked into this blind? I've read every article about your father. I know what people have said, all the conspiracy theories that I'm now thinking are true."

I paused, one sock in hand. "You researched him?"

"Of course I did. When you mentioned who your father was, I spent three nights going down that rabbit hole." He pushed off from the counter and approached me, his expression softening. "We'll get through this together."

"'Together'?" I hated the hope in my voice.

"If you want that."

I melted into his arms again, so damn happy to have him here now. "Yes."

AT OUR FINAL PRE-SEASON GAME AGAINST PHILLY, THIS time at home, I hovered on the edge of the locker room chaos, nerves winding tight in my gut. I didn't talk much to the team—not because I didn't want to, but because I hadn't figured out how to belong yet. But I needed help.

Needed someone. I gritted my teeth, thought of Rebecca's defiant face, and forced myself to speak.

"Does anyone know any good security companies?" I said it louder than I meant to, voice cutting through the chatter like a blade. The room fell abruptly silent, every set of eyes swinging toward me.

Cap was the first to react, rising to stand along with half the team. "You got trouble?" The way he looked, I thought he might go with me to a beat down he was that tense, but then his ex had started dating a soap star and it was all over social media. Hence, why I tried to keep my head down—I'd had enough of being in the spotlight.

"Not for me," I said quickly, shaking my head, not understanding how a team I didn't feel part of was standing up for me. "It's…. it's someone I care about."

Cap studied me for half a second, then gave a curt nod and jerked his thumb toward Noah who wasted no time, circling the logo in the middle of the floor until he was right before me.

"My poppa says he knows people," Noah said without hesitation. "I'll talk to him after practice."

I swallowed hard, gratitude catching me off guard. "Thanks, man. Really."

Noah clapped a hand on my shoulder. "That's what friends are for, right?"

FOURTEEN

Tom

_____

"FIND YOUR CENTER. NOW BREATHE. REMEMBER BREATH IS life. Inhale energy, exhale stress. Now, soften your back as you pull your navel in to touch your spine. Pivot on your back foot as you rise from your lunge into warrior two. Pinkies back, gaze soft, front foot heavy. Now breathe. Feel the power in your hips, glutes, and core as you hold that beautiful Warrior Pose."

"EASY FOR HER TO SAY," I MUMBLED TO WINIFRED WHO gave me a little wag of her stubby tail as she lounged on her mini yoga mat by the window. My girl was spoiled. I fully claimed that and reveled in it. I liked caring for things and people. Was that a crime? Who says big macho men can't be soft inside? So, what if I was a pro football player? Did that mean I couldn't be a caregiver when I wasn't driving a quarterback's ass into the AstroTurf?

Winnie gave me a scolding bark as the morning sun made her black fur glow.

"Sorry. Right. I drifted. Monkey chatter." I collapsed with a huff out of my asana, dropped to the mat, and tucked my legs into a sort-of lotus as I grabbed my phone from the floor to pause the video. Yoga was not my usual stress relief, but I'd already run a few miles and lifted weights. All before seven in the morning. Today was a big day. Huge. It was the day I addressed the nation and told them I was gay. So naturally, sleep had been choppy. Sleep for an hour, then wake up, think, doze off, wake up, think, rinse and fucking repeat. Winnie got up, performed a splendid downward dog pose, and crawled into my lap. I buried my face into her silky fur, so happy to have her back home. Paula had given her over, but with a pout that told me that as soon as she and Ty tied the knot they'd be adopting a dog.

"I'm not so worried about telling everyone on the planet that I'm gay," I told Winnie as we cuddled by the wide window looking over my backyard. I lifted my face from her back to gaze out at the trees. The black gum was already starting to show colors, but the dogwood and maples would be later. It was only the first week of September, but there were subtle signs that fall was just round the corner. "I'm rather relieved about it, to be frank." Winnie sneezed softly. "No, I know your name isn't Frank. It's a human saying." She seemed to accept that explanation, then nudged my hand with her cold nose. "Oh sorry. I stopped petting. So yeah, it's not the fact that I'm telling everyone and their beagle—or cocker—that I like men, it's the happy horseshit that will follow."

And that was what worried me the most. The happy horseshit aka the media feeding frenzy that would, if we weren't extremely careful, find Trick toppling head over tasty ass into the school of piranhas known as the press corp. Also, let us not forget, the internet. Oh, the trolls were going to be trolling like no troll had trolled before. Again, nasty comments online didn't get to me. I generally paid little mind to that shit. I shared things now and again, but my online presence was small other than passing along info about charity events and fundraisers.

My agent, who was now up to drinking two bottles of Mylanta with every meal he liked to remind me, had finally stopped pestering me to be more interactive. Funny that. Now he was all *play it cool* and *keep your head down until the flames die out* amid other pearls of wisdom. I'd keep my head tucked and my eye on the opposing team's QB, play my game, and try to keep Trick on an even keel. As we got closer to my presser, he had grown more and more anxious. Between my schedule and his—our season started today, and his training camp opened in another week or two—we'd not seen much of each other. A few nights here and there, mostly here, as my security was topnotch, and I liked him in my bed.

Winnie gave my still hand another bump. "Oh sorry, girl, I got lost there for a second. Right, so tonight you're going to Grandma's." Her little tail wagged at that. She loved overnighters at my parents'. They spoiled her worse than Paula did, and that was saying something. "I'm sure she will have marrow bones and a new tennis ball. Tomorrow morning, I'll pick you up and bring you home amid, what I am sure, will be hungry newshounds trying to get a bite out of my officially gay backside. What? Well, no, I've been gay since birth, but officially gay as in to the rest of the world."

She looked up at me with a sigh, licked my fingers, and tooted. The smell was atrocious.

"My gods, dog, what have you been eating?" I gagged, placed her on the floor, and shot to my feet as fast as my creaky knees would let me shoot. "Oh right, I fed you the last of my chimichangas last night."

No more refried beans for her. I hurried from my home gym with my dog trotting merrily along behind me, my goal the kitchen and breakfast. Mona had filled the fridge with foods fit for a football player on game day. Lots of eggs, fruits, and a tub of strawberry yogurt. I made myself a shake, some scrambled eggs with a side of turkey bacon, and coffee. Lunch would be after the presser at the stadium, with a light dinner for me before the game. I didn't like being stuffed before I played. I could grab a snack at halftime to keep my energy up and then enjoy something afterward. Something stupidly healthy planned by the team nutritionist focused on fluids for rehydration and good foods to support muscle recovery and rebuild lost energy stores. I'd be lusting for pizza but would settle for what the team provided. I did need to keep my weight in check, but a cheesy meat lover's after a game was the cat's fucking meow.

What I'd love more than sausage, pepperoni, and a bucket of cheese was being able to spend that time with Trick. I sat down with my meal, Winnie crawling into her basket by the fridge to nap whilst also keeping an eye open for any food that might tumble to the floor. A four-legged Rumba charging her batteries. I took a sip of my shake—

not a smoothie thank you, I am a damn football player—and sent Trick a fast good morning text. I knew he would be a mass of emotions today, so thought I could start him off on a good foot.

> Tom: Morning Pucky. I have a joke for you. What do hockey players and magicians have in common? They both do hat tricks. Thank you. Please tip your server. I'll be here all week. *Above typed in Jerry Seinfeld font*

I got no reply all through breakfast, my shower, and my trip to the stadium. As I made my way to the press room, an hour before I needed to be here because I don't know why I was here so fucking early, I sat at the table resting in front of a wall with the team logo of a snarling big cat front and center. I read over the speech my agent had sent me, then I read over the speech the team PR team had sent me, and then I read over the speech I'd scribbled down in Google docs last night at midnight.

My phone buzzed. Texts from the family rolling in as they braced for the flood of questions, comments, and assorted bullshit about to wash over them. My parents had wanted to come, but I'd requested they stay home and release a comment to the press. I'd asked the same of my brothers. I did *not* want them in the spotlight even though they would be pulled into the notoriety regardless. As the time neared for the world to step into my bedroom—and how fucking stupid was it that people had to come out at all—I felt jittery. Ty arrived in a team-branded polo and chinos, very much like I was wearing. After him, a line of my fellow players showed up with various members of the team's upper management. The owner arrived in a suit with a blue tie. I stood up to shake his hand and thank him for his support.

Paul Weiss Luterman was an okay sort. Richer than Croesus, he owned not only a professional football team, but several film studios, as well as a large sporting goods retail chain. Luterman shook my hand firmly, as if expecting my grip to be a little weaker perhaps. Maybe I was just reading into things.

"I'm glad to stand beside you, Tom, as you make your big announcement." He clapped my shoulder and then, took one of the three chairs at the table. Ty and the other Pumas stood off to the sides of the massive room as the press filed in, got some food and drink, and took their assigned seats at several work stations all set up for them with internet access and charging ports. Coach McNair slipped in, gave the media a look that spoke volumes—he was not a fan of the press most days—and then, gave my hand a solid pump before taking seat number two.

My agent was home sick with his double ulcer, but he did text. Most everyone had, even the lady at the doggie daycare where Winnie was at until Paula could pick her up. Everyone had touched in, except Trick. It hurt, but I also understood that he was not ready for any of this yet.

As the press quieted, the owner got to his feet to make a small statement and introduce me. I sat in the middle seat, palms damp, heart racing when my phone vibrated in my back pocket. Slipping it out on the sly, I saw it was from Trick.

Pucky Brewster: Thinking of you on your big day. You are the bravest man I know. I wish I had a tenth of your courage.

He inserted a gold trophy emoji at the end of his message. I smiled down at my phone for a moment, then was gently elbowed by Coach. My gaze flew to the owner, then to the press sitting there, phones out, staring at me.

"Oh, shoot, sorry. I was reading over my speech." I stood up amid soft chuckles from the reporters and sports bloggers. There were a lot in Philly, and I was a big name, so the room was packed. I glanced at Ty, who smiled and gave me a thumbs up, as did all the other Pumas in attendance. Tucker, noticeably, wasn't there. He'd made his feelings known to me for the past week in silent but clear ways. Like ignoring me completely or giving me a wide berth when we had to be close to each other. As if he was scared the gay would rub off. Asshole. "I thought I had what I wanted to say all figured out but, now that I'm looking at all of you, I'm wishing I had studied my notes a little better. My college professors and Coach here will testify to the fact that I tend to skim important things."

Coach nodded. The press smiled politely. "As you know I'm a man of action. I prefer to let my deeds speak for me most of the time. I've always felt that a man is best judged by the things that he holds most dear. For me that has always been football, my family, and my friends. Oh, and dogs, kids, cats, and a few other dozen or so charities. See, I know I got it good. And those who are able to help those in need should. And so, I have. And I plan to continue donating my time and money to those charities after I hang up my cleats at the end of this season."

The press murmured. No one was really shocked to hear me say that. I cleared my throat, looked right at the cameras from several local stations. I wagered the folks wearing lanyards would be a little more wide-eyed after my next announcement.

"Also, I would like to thank my family, my friends, and the coaches that I've known over the years for teaching me how important it is to be honest, not only with yourself, but with the world." I laid my phone down on the table before drawing in a breath, then letting it all go. "After hiding it for my entire life, I have reached a point where I'm tired of hiding who I am. I'll be playing my final season with no more lies clinging to my back. I'll be playing this season as an out gay man. I ask that you respect me, my family, and the team as we head into our first game with a newfound unity and acceptance for every player who calls this organization family."

It took a second for the words to sink in. Then a thousand questions flew at me, but I was already leaving the press room. I was not answering stupid questions. Ty met me in the locker room with a hug that squished the breath from my lungs.

"You did great. So proud of you, man," he said as he squeezed a bit harder before letting go.

I smiled stupidly at the others as they all angled in to ruffle my hair, pat my back, or shake my hand. We had a few moments to talk amongst ourselves before we headed to the owner's box for lunch. A massive spread had been ordered in from the finest eatery on Walnut Street, featuring food that our nutritionist was surely not going to be pleased about. The buffet line formed quickly. I was jabbering with Ty and a few others when my phone gave my butt a buzz.

It was Trick. "Hey, I need to wash up. Don't let Pompano eat all the crab cakes."

The guys laughed. I slipped out of the luxury box and into the nearest bathroom. A unisex toilet that seemed to be quiet for the moment. No way was I going to talk to Trick where anyone could hear me. I pushed in and came face-to-face with Tucker. Well shit. I pocketed my phone and plastered on my most engaging smile.

"Glad to see you could make it. Luterman sprang for prime rib," I said and got a look of pure hatred.

"Did you see the sign on the door?" He looked pretty tight; I could see the tension in his massive shoulders.

"I did."

"Unisex." He spat on the floor beside my spiffy new leather Berluti sneaker. "That's what having a fag on the team brings. Unisex. Men and women sharing the same toilets. It's disgusting, and you are an abomination. I want you to know that decent people do not celebrate a man who fornicates with other men. I will not speak to you or acknowledge your existence, and I shall pray that you get the end that you deserve."

"Well, Bubba, you do what you need to do, just don't slather your hateful shit all over my front door, or I will come after you and it won't be pretty."

"As if I'm scared of a pansy like you."

"Be scared or don't be, just keep to your side of the street, and I'll stay on mine."

"This team is disgusting for allowing a deviate like you anywhere near good decent men. Don't let me catch you looking at me in the shower."

I snorted in amusement. "As if I would want to peek at your shriveled-up dick. We all know how you got so big, Tucker."

His lip curled. "Fag."

He slammed his shoulder into mine as he thundered out of the door. I stood there for a moment, rubbed my shoulder, then pulled some paper towels from the dispenser to clean up the spittle on the floor so whoever came in after me didn't end up on their ass.

I took a moment to reflect on myself in the mirror over the sinks. Funny how I felt the same as I had when he thought I was straight, yet he now hated me solely on who I loved. Guess that made as little sense as not liking a person based on their skin tone or religion. Hatred made no sense no matter what kind or how you looked at it.

Shaking off the explosion of loathing that had slapped me in the face, I rested my ass against a spotless white porcelain sink and tugged my phone free. The text from Trick was short but heartfelt.

> Pucky Brewster: Great speech. Now go out there and show them what kind of chaos a gay football player can bring about.

I thought about texting something stupid back, but I needed to hear his voice to help anchor me in the reality that while some would spit at me, others would embrace me. I'd known I'd get some flack but being spat at and called a slur within an hour of my presser was a bit much.

So, I whispered a prayer to whoever listened to gorillas in cleats that he would be cool talking to me right now. I dialed and I waited for what seemed an eternity for him to pick up.

"Come on, Trick, answer the damn phone."

FIFTEEN

Trick

I ANSWERED THE PHONE IMMEDIATELY.

"Tom," I said, and my voice came out raspy, as if I'd been holding my breath. Maybe I had been. I'd been glued to my phone since the press conference began, watching the livestream with my heart in my throat. "You did it."

"Yeah," he exhaled, and I could hear the mix of relief and tension in his voice. "I did."

"Are you okay?"

"Mostly," he said after a pause. "Just had a run-in with Tucker in the bathroom. Charming guy. Spit at my feet and called me a fag."

My stomach twisted. "Jesus, Tom."

"It's fine," he said quickly, but I could hear the strain. "I expected some pushback. Just maybe not quite so fast or… visceral."

I closed my eyes, leaning against my kitchen counter. The apartment felt too empty, and suddenly, the weight of what Tom was facing hit me all at once. This was what I'd been afraid of—not only for me, but for him. Perhaps his teammate was the first of others alongside opponents and fans.

"You shouldn't have to deal with that shit," I said, gripping the phone tighter, my pulse thudding in my ears. The image of Tom alone in that bathroom, cornered, spat at, wouldn't leave me. I felt a chill of fear crawl down my spine—because what if it got worse? What if next time, it wasn't just words? I hated that he was facing this. I hated that I couldn't protect him. And underneath the fear was guilt, hot and heavy—because he'd stepped into the fire, and I was still hiding in the dark.

"It's nothing I didn't expect," Tom replied, his voice steadier now. "Anyway, enough about that asshole. How are you holding up? You watched it?"

"Every second," I admitted. "You looked good up there. Confident."

"I was terrified," he laughed softly. "Thought I might pass out when the owner handed me the mic."

"Couldn't tell," I said. "You're braver than I am."

There was a pause on the line. "Don't say that Trick." His voice was gentle but firm. "It's not about bravery. It's about timing. You'll know when it's right for you. Hell, it might never be right for you."

"And if I never do? Where does that leave us?"

He hummed, clearly giving it thought. "I'm a great believer in one day at a time."

So, basically he wasn't prepared to go through life as an out gay man while my closeted gay ass clung to his side. I wanted to believe that, someday, I'd stand in front of cameras and say the words that would set me free. But the thought of it made my chest tight, my palms sweaty. The contract I'd signed with my father, the information about my mom, Rebecca—I was buried under all of it.

Change the subject.

"How's the team taking it?"

"Most of them are great. Ty's been my rock, of course. A few others too. The owner's putting on a good show of support, at least to my face." He sighed. "Tucker isn't the only one with issues, but he's the only one stupid enough to say it to my face."

"What happens now?" I asked, pacing my kitchen.

"Now, I go play football," Tom said. "We've got Pittsburgh tonight. I'll focus on the game, block out the noise, and shut people up by racking up sacks."

"Will you be safe?" I couldn't help but ask, as the image of Tucker's anger haunted me. "No one's gonna steamroller you on the field for this? Or not have your back? What about the fans, it's an away, and you're vulnerable out there. Jesus. Why didn't we think this through?"

"We?" he said. "I like that you said 'we'."

"You. I meant you."

"No takebacks. And look, I'm used to being booed, okay? I'll be fine. It's all noise from them and Tucker. Security's been briefed; Coach is all over it; and Ty's got his eyes open." There was a rustling sound, like he was moving. "Listen, I should get back. The team's having lunch before final prep. I just… needed to hear your voice."

The admission made something warm unfurl in my chest. "I'm glad you called."

"Will you watch tonight?" he asked, and I could hear the vulnerability beneath the question.

"Wouldn't miss it." I hesitated, then added softly, "I'll be wearing your jersey."

"You have my jersey?" The surprise in his voice made me smile.

"Yeah," I admitted, feeling heat creep into my cheeks even though he couldn't see me. "Ordered it the day after we first... You know."

His laugh was warm and surprised. "You're full of secrets."

"Just a few." I smiled despite myself. "Go crush it tonight, Tom."

"For you," he whispered. "Watch for me."

"Always."

"Trick?"

"Yep?"

"I like you a lot," Tom said.

I smiled. "I like you, too."

"But do you *like* like me?" Tom asked, and I could hear the smirk in his voice.

"Go win a game, asshole!"

He chuckled, and after we hung up, I stood in my kitchen, clutching the phone to my chest like some lovesick teenager. The enormity of what Tom had done today hit me again—not just coming out, but doing it on his terms, with his head held high. Meanwhile, I was still hiding, still afraid.

I glanced at the clock. Three hours until game time.

Pulling open my closet, I pushed past my Railers gear until I found it—Tom's blue and gold Pumas jersey,

FULKOWSKI emblazoned across the back. I'd worn it only in private but tonight felt different. Tonight, I needed to be close to him, even if only in spirit.

My phone buzzed again—Rebecca this time, from the burner I'd made her get. I still hadn't told her that messaging Noah's father meant there was now security following her every movement—probably best that I left that for a while because I can guarantee that is going to blow up in my face.

Secrets.

Until I figured things out.

> Rebecca: Tom Fulkowski came out! It's all over social media.

Trick: I saw.

In a moment of madness, I wanted to share my pride with Rebecca. I wasn't sure how to italicize text and stared at my phone momentarily before deciding asterisks were okay.

Trick: I'm so proud of him and also, I think I * like * like him.

> Rebecca: Wait.

> Rebecca: What?

> Rebeccas: Is he the guy? YOUR guy?

Trick: Yeah. He is.

Three dots appeared, disappeared, and appeared again.

Rebecca: Holy shit, Trick. Wow. You okay?

Trick: I think so. I'm watching his game tonight.

Rebecca: You going to buy his jersey?

She added a winking emoji, and I sent back rolling eyes.

Trick: Already wearing it.

Rebecca: You want company?

I felt immediate fear—that my father knew where I was staying, that he'd see Rebecca arrive, and he'd ruin her life, but then it hit me, she was in Pittsburgh, I was in Harrisburg.

Rebecca: We can video call and watch it together

My relief was instant.

Trick: I'd love that

Rebecca: Get snacks, I'll meet you at the warmups

Rebecca: Then we can both admire football player butts

Rebecca: Mmmm, those tight pants

WE ENDED UP ON VIDEO CALL, I WAS PROPPED ON THE couch, she was tucked under a blanket with a massive bowl of popcorn. The commentary was already wild— Tom had pulled off a sack within the ten-yard line, leaving the other team—and quarterback—flat-footed.

Rebecca whooped. "Did you see that?! Who does that?"

"Tom," I said, my voice low, warm. "Looking sexy as hell doing it."

She laughed. "I can't believe you're the romantic one in this sibling duo."

"Shut up and watch the game."

The Pumas were up 24–21, but it was tight, the fourth quarter winding down. Every time the camera cut to Tom —eyes locked in, mouthguard clenched—I couldn't help it. My heart thumped harder.

Rebecca glanced at me through the screen. "You're a goner."

Two minutes on the clock. The other team had just scored again—24–28 now—and the Pumas had one last drive to turn it around. The commentators were breathless, the tension rising with every snap of the ball.

Tom took to the field as though he owned it—calm and collected, that same mouthguard clenched between his teeth. Pittsburgh first down. Complete. Second down. A rush for four. Third down. And then—magic. The opposing QB dropped back, dodged a tackle, rolled left, pump-faked, and nothing. A big-bodied defender—my defender—was now inches from him. The crowd groaned in unison when Tom slapped the ball from the quarterback's hand. Tom leapt on the fumble, scooping it up like a loaf of bread, and then broke free. Stiff-armed, he held off an offensive lineman as he ran as fast as he could, diving into the end zone.

Touchdown.

The place exploded.

Rebecca shrieked so loudly that I flinched. "What even was that?"

I was laughing, breathless. "That was my guy."

The Pumas closed it out 31–28, and when the camera zoomed in on Tom, helmet off, hair damp, grinning like a man who'd saved the world—I couldn't take my eyes off him.

"You're so gone on him," she said when we said goodnight.

Yeah. I really fucking was.

MY SPORTS LAWYER, CYNTHIA CHO, WAS AN ALL-AROUND decent human being. Her dark hair pushed up in a messy bun somehow made her look more capable, and she sat behind a practical desk, not a fancy one with gold trim. There were no bible verses on her wall, just evidence of her law degree, and a roll call of her clients, five of whom played for the Railers. There was no laptop, only a legal pad, and she had a quiet kind of competence that made me finally exhale. I'd hired her after I joined the Railers. She didn't flinch at my reputation; she negotiated with steel and made things happen, even if I came in with baggage.

But this wasn't about hockey. And it definitely wasn't going to be easy.

"You may not be able to help me," I said, still standing. "This isn't about my contract with the Railers. This is personal."

"I might not be best placed. I'm not family law, but if you want to explain, I have a colleague I can call. Sit down."

I slumped into the chair she pointed at. Fear gripped me. "And everything is confidential."

"Always."

"*And* you know who my father is."

She wrinkled her nose as if she'd bitten into something sour, but the expression vanished quickly. "Cole Harrington II. Televangelist Pastor."

"I'm trusting you with this, but I need help."

"Pregnancy? Drugs? DUI?"

My mouth fell open. "God no. None of the above. I know you won't be able to help, but I needed to tell someone, and—"

"Spit it out, Mr. Harrington, surprise me."

"Call me Trick, please." I passed her my copy of the emancipation deal I'd signed at sixteen. "My father's people handled this. I wish I could say I didn't know what I was signing, but I did. I knew that if I didn't sign, they'd release information about what they called my deviancies, and I'd never have the chance to get away, and worse, things about my mom that would put her suicide front and center."

She didn't flinch, only nodding as she listened, not looking at the contract.

"Half of everything I make goes to the ministry. And my agent, again connected to my father, of course, takes his cut. It's all buried under 'spiritual guidance' and legacy funds and whatever bullshit label they use to keep it clean."

Cynthia reached for her pad and began to make notes. "What do you need from me?"

"I have a sister. I didn't know I had one. But…" I passed her the envelope Rebecca had given me. "… it's all in there. Proof she's my sibling. I want out of the emancipation contract. I want my will changed. I want everything to go to Rebecca. I want to protect her from my father, because he's threatening her if she contacts me or goes public. There's been some big money paid over the years to her mom." I rubbed my eyes. "It's so twisted up, I don't know where to start, but I have many reasons to get my house in order."

Tom. Coming out. Starting over.

"I want the contract voided. I want a clean break. Can you help me?"

She glanced up, then gave me a sharp nod.

"Let's talk about the legal status first," she said. "In most states, a minor can be emancipated at sixteen, but only through a formal court process. That typically requires proving you can support yourself financially, live independently, and that emancipation is in your best interest. If your emancipation was tied to a private contract instead of a court order, we might already have grounds to challenge it."

I blinked. "So, it's not necessarily legal?"

"Even if you were granted emancipation legally, no contract—especially one signed under duress or with coercion—is unbreakable. Blackmail, threats, or misinformation make that contract vulnerable. We can argue undue influence, lack of capacity, or fraudulent inducement."

"Even though I knew what I was signing?"

"Even then," she said, eyes sharp. "A sixteen-year-old pressured into forfeiting half their earnings under the threat of personal exposure and family trauma? That's coercion. We go through the discovery process, find the paper trail, the threats, the manipulation. And if your father's ministry used this to enrich itself, it could violate multiple financial laws."

"There's a way out if I'm brave enough to take it?" *I want to be brave.*

"There's always a way out." She went to the door and called for someone to join us, a balding man with a broad smile.

"Big fan," he said by way of introduction. "Mark Lewis."

"Hi."

Cynthia gestured for Mark to sit. "Emancipation. Sixteen. Shit contract," she said.

Mark almost rubbed his hands with glee. "Wow. For real?" He spun his chair. "Let's get this party started."

SIXTEEN

Tom

Sometimes fate gave you a gift.

This weekend, the first of November, was a blessing delivered from on high. By whatever forces moved people about on this little blue and green rock, Trick and I had games in the same town on the same weekend. We'd not been able to sneak in any personal time for weeks with his travel schedule warring with mine. This weekend, we were in Philly. I had a home game at one on Sunday against Washington, and Trick was playing tonight against our team. Talk about being torn about which jersey to wear. I ended up chickening out and pulling on a hoodie from a local LGBTQ charity, while Ty wore a Philly jersey.

I may have pulled some strings to get us tickets by the glass beside the Railers bench. Being a big name did have its perks. Ty and I had been shown on the Jumbotron already, and we had barely sat down. The applause for us had been boisterous, which helped soften the slings and arrows from haters who had been peppering me with abuse ever since I'd come out. The fans surrounding us had shaken hands and gotten selfies right off the bat. Again, nice to know most people were decent.

"You're going to freeze," Ty said as he placed his extra-large cup of root beer on the ledge by the Plexiglas. I tucked my drink down between my feet while drooling over my cheesesteak. You didn't do a sporting event in this city and not have a cheesesteak or one of our famous soft pretzels. People had been tossed into the Delaware for less.

"Nah, I'm good." That was a lie. The singer was belting out the anthem and my nipples were hard enough to cut through the glass separating us from the ice. "I got a coat."

We took our seats as the teams met at center ice. The Railers had been having a pretty good season so far. Tied for second in their division. The Pumas had been ripping things up over the past few Sundays and were in first place with what looked to be an easy game this Sunday. Of course, it never paid to get too cocky. Any team can win on any given day as coaches are known to say.

"Okay, whatever, man. So, fill me in as we go. Three periods, right?" I nodded while he dipped a chunk of soft pretzel into a cup of melted cheese. Tyrese was here to meet Trick after the game because I wanted to introduce my best friend to the man who had won my heart. Yes, Trick knew I had confided to Ty about our relationship. I'd discussed it with him at length, and he had been okay with Ty and Paula knowing. We were going to do a brunch at Pestoni Brothers on Rittenhouse Square tomorrow. Top-notch eatery with a fabulous menu. It was our first time out with another couple. The meet-up tonight was to ease Trick into the brunch Paula had planned for tomorrow.

And while Trick and I couldn't act like a *couple,* just being out with him in public with two of the most important people in my world outside of my family was huge. I was ecstatic. Trick was cautious. I was sure it would all be fine.

After a short beer with Ty at a bar across the street from the arena tonight, then we—Trick and I—I'd have him in my bed for a whole night, and the next morning before we did brunch. Sadly, Trick had to fly out from PIA for a road trip out west, so this one night was all we would have for another couple of weeks. Then, it was Thanksgiving. Thank God we weren't playing on the holiday and neither was Trick, so I was trying to convince him to come to my parents' for the big meal. It was a work in progress, but he seemed interested in seeing where I'd grown up and meeting the people who'd raised me, yet he was hesitant at the same time. I'd keep working on him. I had mighty persuasive ways.

"Okay, so Trick is that one. Damn! Oh man. That puck moves!" Ty shouted as the Railers came steaming into the Philly end zone. Noah Gunnersson took a shot on goal. It hit the pipe with a clatter that made everyone in the arena go YAAAYY. The puck flew off the goal into the corner. Six men converged on that spot. The little black disc wiggled out of the group, then skittered along until one of our hometown guys got to it and the action streaked down to the other end. "Mm, man they are fast. I see it now. Like on TV it doesn't look this speedy, but in person—Oh! Shit, that was close. Oh!" He shot to his feet, pretzel dripping cheese onto his sneakers when a fight broke out by the Railers net. "Hit him!! Oh damn. Oh shit. Did you see that?! That's a penalty. What?! Why is our guy going to the box, too?!" Fans nearby leaned in to explain what was going on, and what roughing and embellishment meant. "Okay, so doing a big flip after a guy taps you on the shoulder is showing off. Man, this is crazy. What, so now they play four-on-four. I get why people love this game now. Oh shit, my sneaker!"

He sat, then bent over to scrub the cheese off his sneaker. Trick and his line were out now. They won the faceoff. Tensions on the benches were high. The Railers had been yelling at our Philly players steadily since the penalties. When one of our players stole the puck from Trick, he got hot. It was sexy as hell. He skated over and checked the guy into the boards. I jumped back at the impact. The glass rattled dangerously. Ty got a soaking as his root beer flew off the ledge and dumped into his lap.

I laughed so hard I was sure I had wet my pants. Ty was a good sport about it after we got his hair dried with cheesy napkins. One of the guys behind us ran off to get Ty another root beer, which was damn nice. This time, he placed it between his feet. Lesson one of what *not* to do at a hockey game had been learned. I couldn't wait to tell Trick about it. Right after I loved him all over of course. Man had to have his priorities.

———

WHEN TRICK LAY PANTING AND SPENT BESIDE ME, HIS sweet bubble butt pink from my whiskers, I slapped my hands to my heaving chest and smiled proudly at the ceiling over my bed. Not only had I wrung two orgasms from the puck pusher, but I'd also gotten him to admit that my dick was truly phenomenal. Of course, he had yelled that about my dick as he had been riding it, but the compliment stays.

"Holy hell," he huffed as he eased to his side, arm pillowing his head. "I think you broke me."

"Sweet-talker," I replied, then sat up, slowly, to stare at the bedroom door. Winnie lay on the other side whining ever so gently. "You okay if I let the dog in? She always sleeps with me when I'm home and hearing her crying is making me sad inside."

"Marshmallow," he mumbled as he rolled off the bed. "Sure, but let's get washed up first, okay?"

Yeah, that sounded good. One fantastic blowjob from Trick, followed by a hot shower later, we were wrapped up in my duvet, a black cocker spaniel snoring indelicately by our feet, holding each other as the night grew colder outside. There would be frost on my jack-o-lanterns in the morning. Poor things. I'd have the gardeners chuck them into the compost bin.

"God you feel so good in my bed." I sighed as we cuddled close, his breath warm on my chest, his fingers moving through the pelt of hair on my chest. "I wish I could have you here every night." I yawned sleepily. He murmured something into my pec that I didn't catch over the ladylike snores floating up from my dog. "What, baby?"

"Said that would be nice," he whispered, then lifted his cheek from where it had been resting over my heart to gaze at me softly. "I like your bed, and your dog, and your friend. He will be discreet?"

"Absolutely. Ty is one of the best humans on this planet. You'll love Paula too. She's so bright, so funny, and so pretty."

"Okay, yeah, I want to meet her, and your family, I'm just…"

I gave his cheek a stroke with the back of my big, fat fingers. "I know and it's all good. Don't push yourself too hard. I can be a bit of a pushy dick at times, but I just have so much that I want to share with you, Trick. I love you."

His eyes flared. A jolt of panic hit me square in the chest. Damn my big mouth. I'd been so careful to keep my emotions in check, not an easy thing for me, and now I'd blown everything to fucking bits. He'd freak out, run off, and we'd have to start all over again, if he would even see me at all. Fuck. God, I was an asshole of the highest caliber.

"What did you say?" His voice was smooth as the fur on a puppy belly.

"Trick, I meant that I—"

"No, don't make things up. Say it again." His gaze was intense.

Fearing what I had done, I wet my lips and spoke the words again. "I love you."

He seemed to become lost in himself for the longest moment I had ever experienced. It took all the resolve I possessed not to tighten my hold on him. He would run. I knew it. My battered brainpan was already spinning out wild ways to try to win him back when he blinked away whatever mental soup he had been splashing about in.

"You love me." Not a question but a statement.

"I do. Madly. Wildly. With all my heart."

In for a penny as they say…

He could only streak off into the night once.

"That's…" He cleared his throat. Winnie snuffled. The chilly November winds blew outside as they carried the first taste of winter into my yard and possibly my heart as well. "That's powerful."

"Yeah, I know. We can shelve that for later. I never meant to say it, I was just—"

He brushed a kiss over my lips. "I love you, too." Now it was my turn to gape like a dunderhead. "That's the dopey football face I know and love."

"Wait." My heart was skipping. "You said it twice."

"Yeah, I did." He stared at me with a trace of fear in his gaze. "I'm not good at this. I don't know what a normal relationship is, so when I fuck things up, be patient."

"Trick, baby, I am sure you'll be fine. It's me being all needy and clingy that will fuck things up."

"No, it'll be me."

"Nope me. Big dumb football player will hose things up."

Trick opened his mouth to counter when Winnie yipped at us in a most aggravated way. We both fell silent as the dog sniffed haughtily, stood up, walked in a circle four times, and then lay down with a resigned sigh.

"I think that was doggy for stop arguing and just kiss each other," I whispered, then did just that. I kissed the ever-loving daylights out of the man that I loved, who loved me back.

Guess sometimes you need a third party to tell you to stop angsting and cuddle. Even if that third party was a cocker spaniel.

RITTENHOUSE SQUARE IS ONE OF THE FIVE ORIGINAL SQUARES laid out by the city planner William Penn back in the late seventeenth century. It's the heart of Center City Philadelphia. Close by you can find fine dining, luxury retail shops, and some of the city's most exclusive apartments. This tree-filled park is named after David Rittenhouse, an astronomer and clockmaker. Mr. Rittenhouse was the first director of the US Mint and a public official, as well as a member of the American Philosophical Society. As you enjoy the park, you can take note of some of the famous statues such as Lion Crushing a Serpent by Antoine-Louis Brye, which sits in the central plaza.

As I stood staring at said sculpture, Trick yanked my ear bud from my ear. I glanced over to see his cheeks were red as apples and his nose was running. He was adorable. I really wanted to kiss him, but I didn't dare.

"This is all really fascinating," he said as he wiped at his nose with a hankie. I turned off the walking tour narrative I'd rented for us to enjoy.

"You think so?" I asked as joggers moved around us— breath steaming, scarves tight around their necks.

"No, to be honest, if I wasn't shaking so damn hard, I would have fallen asleep by that goat statue."

"Ah." Okay, so this was a bust. Maybe in the summer when the trees and flowers were all out and being glorious. "Yeah, got it. We're a little early, but we can head to the restaurant."

I was pretty hungry. Making love to your man all night will do that to a guy.

"Cool." He hunkered down into his coat, shoulders up around his ears. I had forgotten he was a Southern boy. Even though he spent a lot of time on the ice, he was exerting himself while skating, so he was rarely cold.

I nearly grabbed his hand but fisted mine instead. Nope. *No touchy-feely boyfriend stuff, Thomas.* Not that we had used the BF term, but after sharing our feelings last night, I felt it was safe to call him that in my head. So, instead of holding hands, I shouldered him through the park and into Pestoni Brothers. The waiting area was packed, and as we were early, our table wasn't ready, so we moseyed along on the heels of a beautiful young man dressed in the Pestoni black slacks, green shirt, and black vest to the bar.

We had gotten our mocktail mimosas when Ty and Paula arrived. They joined us at the bar, and introductions were made. Paula was wearing a gray sweater dress and looked incredible. She and Trick hit it right off. She was a whiz at getting people to open up, a trait that would serve her well in a law career. They were jabbering about a new movie they'd both seen. Something scary. I didn't do horror. I hated jump scares almost as much as I hated athlete's foot, and I hated that fungus *a lot.*

The eatery was packed with the upper class of Philadelphia society. The rich and famous all made it a point to nod, wave, or when we were seated, stop by our table, which looked out at the chilly park we had walked through. Ty and I were polite, as always. Trick and Paula had fallen back into discussing another movie that I would never see when the city's managing director dropped by our table to chat.

Marcus Berry was a tall man with a soft chin, fair skin with old acne scars, and a receding hairline. He'd been appointed by the new mayor last year and loved Puma football.

"Nice to see you again,","" I said as I shook hands with Marcus.

He waved his wife on to their table as he began to dig into his jacket for something. I hoped it might be a handkerchief, as he had the sweatiest palms of any man with whom I had ever had the misfortune of shaking hands. Ty didn't need to suffer the sweat. But no, Marcus pulled out his cell phone and showed me a grainy picture as he began to blather on about what a small world it was seeing me and Trick together, yet again. I threw a glance at Trick, who was now engaged in whatever Marcus pattering on about at high speed as his name had been mentioned. "I'm sorry, but I'm not sure exactly—"

"This picture. It's all over the internet. Seems some guy who owns a putt-putt golf just sold it to some tabloid." I grabbed at his phone to bring it closer to my nose. Well shit. There we were, me and Trick, playing fucking golf way back in the summer. It was nothing scandalous. Just two men trying to putt a golf ball past a pirate's peg leg. "Guess he said he didn't think anything of it before, but then you came out as gay and he got to thinking. Maybe Tom and that guy were here on a date. And now, here we see you out in public again. It's just funny isn't it? Are you two dating? Not that I mind at all! I'm elbow-deep in planning next year's Pride event. We love our LGBTQ friends!"

I released the cell and chanced a look at Trick. He appeared as if he was one meow shy of having kittens.

"It doesn't mean a thing, Trick," I whispered after Ty, sensing something on the wind, escorted the confused managing director to his table. "Seriously, it's just us playing golf. No long looks or telling touches. Two friends out doing buddy stuff."

"No, it's more than that, Tom. He'll make the connection. He'll see us out in public twice and know what is going on. Everyone will know."

I glanced around the packed restaurant. No one was paying us any mind now. Trick was just overreacting.

Then, Ty sat back down. He did *not* appear happy. "You two are all over the internet. Golf Guy started it, but then, someone in the park shared a picture of you two looking cozy while checking out the *Duck Girl* statue. And then, someone just dropped a shot from here of you and Trick at the bar sipping drinks and whispering to each other."

"Whispering? We were just talking softly as people do at a fine restaurant!" I growled, throwing a dark glare at my fellow diners. Who the hell here had jumped on that stupid bandwagon so quickly? "We're just two friends having brunch with two more friends. Since when is it something salacious for two friends to do things together?"

"When one is famous and comes out," Trick said as his cell phone started to buzz steadily. He flipped it over on the table. "The fuck?"

"What?"

"Media shit."

Suddenly, I wasn't ravenous anymore.

SEVENTEEN

Trick
———

I WAS STILL IN SHOCK.

Dinner had been good—so good it felt like a dream I didn't deserve. Tom and Ty had cracked jokes across the table, slinging friendly insults about football versus hockey while I laughed more in an hour than I had in an entire month. Paula was simply delightful. Tom had sat close, his knee brushing mine under the table, and I hadn't moved. Not even when he reached past me for the pepper grinder and his hand landed on my shoulder, light as a whisper.

It was nothing.

It was everything.

That single point of contact meant more than it should have. Not because it was overtly romantic or intentional. But because it was him. Tom. And for a breathless moment, it felt as if he *saw* me. Not the player, the problem, or the one carrying a secret like a curse. Just me. And I wanted to lean into it. Into him. Into something that didn't feel like shame. I imagined we could navigate this world and still keep our privacy, but I'd been naïve. Those fucking photos made it *something*. I shouldn't have looked. But I did. When I was in Tom's car heading back to his place, I read some of the comments. Each word hit like a punch to the gut. My throat tightened as I scrolled, hands trembling, the screen swimming in the dim light. I could hear my pulse in my ears, feel the heat rise up the back of my neck as if I'd been caught doing something shameful. It wasn't only the words—they were cruel, yes —but it was the knowing. The confirmation of every fear I'd buried under years of control. That people were watching. Judging. Picking apart my life like vultures with viral hashtags and gossip.

My chest clenched. I felt like I was sixteen again, staring down a Bible and a punishment I never deserved. I should throw the phone across the car, but instead, I kept reading. Like a masochist. *Tomrick* was trending.

"Tom and Trick's gay love?"

"Abomination."

"What's in the water in Harrisburg?"

"No wonder Atlanta traded his ass!"

It didn't matter that I wasn't out and had done nothing to warrant the comments. A couple of photos. A couple of smiles. That was all it took for people to start drawing lines and assumptions and dragging me out of a closet I'd boarded shut. I'd built that closet with blood and bone. Brick by silent brick. And now it was splintering under the weight of someone else's camera lens.

Tom drove us back to his place in silence. His jaw was tight, his eyes on the road, his shoulders coiled as if he were waiting for a blow. He had every right to be worried about himself and what this might mean for the peaceful, quiet life he'd only just begun to reclaim. This was my fault—my mess, my ruin, bleeding into his fresh start. I'd been so young when my father had dragged me into that place with soft lighting, softer voices, and promises wrapped in prayer. They said I was confused. Sick. Possessed. They said I could be saved. What they really meant was, they'd break me into pieces and call the splinters healed. When I'd finally gotten out—after handing over a signed NDA and half my fucking future income—they'd smiled. Told me I was fixed. I'd walked away empty. Hollow. As if love had been surgically removed and shame stitched into its place.

I will come out. One day. When it's safe. I'm sure pieces of me will survive. But the world was watching. Judging. And I was cracking under the weight of trying to hide.

Tom's street blurred into view—and so did the flashing cameras. People clustered at the gate like wolves in designer jackets. We rolled through, then the gates closed behind us, but the flashes kept coming. I turned my face, ducked down, nausea clawing up my throat. When the garage door shut and sealed us inside, I stumbled from the car, my knees nearly buckling. *I can't breathe.* Panic surged—raw, blinding. My chest heaved as if my lungs had forgotten how to work. I backed up, shaking, my hands trembling at my sides. Tom moved toward me. Slow. Careful.

He touched my chest, right over my heart—and I shattered. Just from that. Then, his mouth was on mine, a kiss in the dark, desperate and trembling as if we were fugitives clinging to a moment of stolen peace. When I pulled back, I was breathless. Broken open. I couldn't stay. I climbed into my car and left. No glance back.

I didn't blast music. Didn't speed. I drove with both hands on the wheel, eyes fixed on the night, trying to outrun the ache. Somewhere outside Harrisburg, I pulled into the shadowed corner of a fast food parking lot and killed the engine. The silence felt like drowning.

"God made man and woman in His image…"

"What you're feeling isn't love…"

"You're not special. You're sick. But we can help you…"

And fuck, I *had* wanted help. After Mom died, when it was only him and me left, I wanted to be loved. I wanted to be *enough*. It was easier to let them fix me than to keep breaking. So, I let them baptize me again. Not because I believed them. Not really. But I was so desperate to feel clean again, to be something they could love—something *he* could love—that I let them drown me in holy water and call it healing. Part of me had hoped it would work. The rest of me had simply wanted to survive. Wanted the silence. The approval. Even if it came at the cost of who I was. I sat in their circles. I spoke the words they wanted. I nodded, smiled, and signed my future away just to *escape*.

My phone screen lit up, and it snagged my attention—only two people were on this chat, Rebecca and Tom.

Rebecca: Are you there?

A string of messages. Growing more anxious. More real. I wiped my face, then hit call, and she answered instantly.

"Trick?" Her voice cracked. "Thank fuck! Just ignore it all. It's just noise."

I didn't know her well enough yet, but in that moment, I felt I did. I imagined growing up with her instead of with sermons and silence—a life with a sister instead of a doctrine. Maybe then, I wouldn't be so goddamn broken. My head dropped to the wheel. And I sobbed. The kind of sobs that broke loose from somewhere deep and ancient. My chest caved in with the force of it, and I couldn't catch my breath, couldn't stop shaking. I gasped through each jagged inhale, fingers clawing at the steering wheel like it could anchor me to something real. My whole body ached —not from pain, but from the sheer release. Years of holding it together had finally ruptured in the safety of that one moment. Rebecca talked me through it, stayed on the line, her voice steady.

"I'm sorry," I said on one last sob.

"You *never* have to be sorry with me. You don't deserve any of this shit, not Pastor Cole, not your secrets, none of it."

Her words cracked something open inside me again. "You don't know what I deserve."

"You *deserve* love."

I sat in silence, staring out at nothing. "This isn't fair to you or Tom," I muttered. "I'm just—damaged. I don't even know who I am outside of all this shit in my head. You should back away before I drag you down with me."

"Nope," she said, firm and soft. "You've got me now, Trick. For life. We'll figure it out together."

We talked until I could breathe, but when the call ended, it was three in the morning, and I wasn't ready to go home. Hell, I didn't know what I *was* ready for. Somehow, I ended up in front of Noah and Brody's place. I hadn't meant to go there. My hands had taken me. Maybe my heart had, too.

I pulled off the road, engine cooling with slow metallic clicks, and leaned my forehead against the wheel.

"Now what?" I whispered.

A knock on the window scared the shit out of me. I jerked upright, heart pounding, and peered out into the dark, where a flashlight beam cut through the shadows—then another tap, gentler this time.

"Trick?" Noah called through the window, sporting a worried expression, his breath visible in the night air. He tucked the flashlight under his arm and rapped again on the glass. "Are you okay?" he asked as I rolled the window down a crack.

I swallowed hard. "What are you doing out here?"

"I could ask you the same. Our security service notified us that someone was loitering outside."

"Jesus, Gunny, call the cops next time. I could have been anyone."

"Nah, Brody recognized your car."

"He did?"

Noah huffed. "Of course he did; that man knows cars, but that's unimportant. Look, I've opened the gate—come on, drive in. Coffee's on."

When I entered their property, Brody was waiting in pajama pants and a hoodie with Gunny's number on the back, quietly closing the gate behind me. He gave a sleepy wave, then disappeared inside to give us space. I parked next to the Ferrari and climbed out, hugging my arms around myself. "I'm sorry to be here at…" I glanced at my watch. "Jesus, it's the middle of the fucking night."

"It's all good," Noah said, leading the way to the porch. We stepped into the warmth of the house, the scent of coffee already threading through the air. Noah handed me a mug without a word and gestured toward the couch.

"Do you want to talk about it?" he asked softly as we sat. "I mean, I saw the photos, and all the crap that they're saying, which is just bullshit, Trick, okay? Having a friend doesn't make you gay; photos don't prove you're gay."

I didn't answer right away. The coffee warmed my hands, but the tightness in my chest hadn't eased. He threw me his stupid big smile all tousled with his stupid blond curls and his Mr. Nice Guy awesomeness, and everything tumbled out of me in a flash.

"I'm gay, Noah. And I'm in a relationship with Tom Fulkowski."

Noah stared at me, eyes wide, then gave me a sharp nod. "Okay then."

My throat closed. I sipped the coffee. Let the silence settle. Noah didn't push. He sat beside me, quiet and steady, and for the first time in hours, I didn't feel like I was falling.

"I don't know what to do next."

Did I stay quiet and hope the noise faded, or did I step into the fire and own it all? Did I contact my lawyer, call the team management, did I come out, did I fix this, or did I keep driving until I was well away from my life? Every option felt like a gamble I wasn't ready to take. But I couldn't sit in this limbo forever without losing even more of myself.

Noah leaned back, watching me carefully over the rim of his mug. "Are you coming out? Or do you want to deflect? What can we do to help?"

I stared into the coffee as if it held the answers. "Nothing. Unless you know a therapist who can fix my head." Without missing a beat, Noah tugged his phone closer. Seconds later, my cell vibrated on the table.

"Louisa Mathers," he said. "She's amazing. Brody talked to her."

I didn't ask what Brody had talked to her about. "I'll call her in the morning," I muttered, voice rough.

Noah nodded. "You're not alone, Trick. And whatever you decide to do, it's *your* decision, on *your* timeline. Brody and I have your back."

I closed my eyes for a second, breathing in the smell of coffee and safety, and let the truth of that settle over me like a blanket I didn't know I needed. "I need to call Tom."

He smiled, then took his cup to the sink. "Stay here tonight. Spare room with a bathroom, top of the stairs. I'll open the door so you can see it and throw some Railers stuff in there for you to wear. Talk to Tom down here." He clapped a hand on my shoulder. "You've got this."

I waited until Noah disappeared upstairs before pulling out my phone and calling Tom. It rang once, and then he answered.

"Trick?" His voice was bright as if he hadn't been sleeping.

"I'm sorry I left," I said, my voice cracking. "I'm a mess. I couldn't breathe. I talked to Rebecca, and now I'm at Noah's. I didn't mean to come here, but... I guess I couldn't face the rental. I told him that I was gay, and that you and me…" My voice cracked. "… Did I fuck it up? Is there still a you and me?"

Tom sighed. "Very definitely a you and me, babe."

I took a breath. "I don't know what happens next. Everything feels out of control, but I know for sure I love you."

Another pause.

Then Tom said, "I love you, too. We'll ride this storm, ignore the shit online. What happened doesn't mean you need to dignify any of it with a response. When you're ready, we'll make it public and live our lives one day, but I understand it might be after you're done playing, Trick. Okay? I'm not going anywhere."

I was nodding, belatedly realizing he wouldn't be able to see. "I can't ask you to do that, not when you've come out—"

"That's my choice."

"No, Tom, I want to tell the world who I am, but not today, not like this. I need to talk to my lawyers, sign the new wills to pass everything to Rebecca, stop the payments to my father, get my head fixed. Shit, that's a lot. But I'll do it, for Rebecca, for you, and me. For *us*." I felt immediately lighter because it was almost as if I was making a plan. "I need to mend what's in my head. Or at least give it space for me to think properly."

"Anything you need, I'm here."

"I know. And I have the biggest incentive to get myself on an even keel."

"Love?"

"Well, duh, but also… if you think I'm missing out on

Thanksgiving dinner with your family, you're out of your mind."

We both laughed at that—an honest, helpless kind of laughter, not forced, but warm. A tiny crack of light breaking through the storm clouds I'd been carrying. For the first time in what felt like forever, I believed that maybe I could be myself. I felt nauseous and panicked at the thought, not even sure who I was, but it was a step in the right direction.

"We'll figure it out," Tom said gently. "Day by day. You and me."

"Yeah," I whispered. "You and me."

EIGHTEEN

Tom
_____

NEVER DID TWO MEN EVER NEED COMFORT FOOD MORE than Trick and I did.

To say the past couple of weeks had been akin to taking a stroll through the seventh and eighth rings of hell would have been close to the Mount St. Helen's worthy explosion of shit that had rained down not only on Trick and I, but on our teams as well.

The Pumas hadn't exactly been expecting a romance—alleged, I had pointed out several dozen times—quite so quickly. Not having the base of knowledge of how to handle that sort of flood, my team sort of fumbled the ball a few times until I was forced to address things. I'd kindly told the press what Trick had asked me to tell them. That Trick and I had met while working with BoltFuel—who were still eerily quiet about us being involved with their product, but oh well—and became friends. I had also added that it was entirely possible for a gay man to have male friends and not be fucking them. Yes, I had dropped the F-bomb. The Puma PR team birthed a squad of mooselings, but the message was delivered. Firmly. After that little tidbit of profanity, the bro dudes backed off. Maybe some of the straights just needed to be reminded that you could be friends with the sex you were attracted to. Or, maybe, my FAFO face while I had made my little speech had intimidated the het boys. Hell, maybe they were impressed that I had told it like it was. Whatever the case, things began to settle. A blessing for Trick, who was juggling a dozen personal balls while trying to concentrate on hockey.

It wasn't easy to focus on your sport when people were deluging you with stupid shit from left, right, front, and center. The Railers stood by Trick without being as glaringly crude about it as I had been. They had lots of experience dealing with queer players. The Pumas would learn. Maybe my team needed to steal Layton Foxx from the Railers.

So, now that we had the world convinced—mostly maybe—that we were only friends, our lives could go on normally. And on Thanksgiving, that meant family and food. The start of the family part was welcoming Trick's sister Rebecca into my home. She had arrived last night, won Winnie over instantly, and had charmed me wholly. Trick was different around her. Softer, gentler, less prone to snark. I enjoyed seeing it. He desperately needed the support a sibling offered. And I really needed a sister. I had adopted her into my heart the moment she kissed Winnie.

Now, I was waiting for my new sister—yes, she would legally be my sister-in-law someday, but I wasn't tossing that at Trick just yet—to join us in the living room so we could drive to my parents' house.

"Is she always this late?" I asked Trick while checking my smart watch for the tenth time in five minutes.

"I'm not sure. We just met."

Oh yeah. "Well, I could say something sexist—"

"I wouldn't," Rebecca said as she rushed down the stairs with Winifred on her heels. She looked pretty in a soft white blouse, dark brown slacks, and a jazzy vest with gold threading.

"You're making us look like slobs," I said as she twirled around the room, Winnie dancing on her back legs. Guess my girl had also been craving another female. Trick and I were wearing clean jeans topped with polos.

"Someone has to represent," she said, then paraded past us as she pulled on a sleek winter coat.

I looked at Trick. He shrugged, but his smile was tight. Even with his sister along, he was nervous about meeting my family. I'd told him over and over that they were just ordinary folks. My brothers were goobers. The food would rock his world. We'd eat; we'd talk; we'd fall asleep in front of the TV for the Dallas/NY game. Poor slobs. I was thrilled to not be playing today. Ratings be damned. A soul needed family, and Trick and I had exceptionally weary souls of late.

"I bet I slobber gravy on the front of my shirt before you do," I commented as we began bundling up for the ride over the bridge to Philly. Winnie wore her little snow boots and a matching mint green coat. A few inches of fresh snow had fallen on the east yesterday. The roads were fine, but the lawns were crunchy. Winnie had very delicate pads. The snow built up between her toes, which made her uncomfortable, so booties it was.

"Probably," Trick replied as he shrugged into his coat.

I gave him a quick kiss. He blushed deep red as his sister made silly kissy sounds behind us. I was used to sibling teasing. Trick wasn't, but he broke free from me, then rolled his eyes at both of us before snapping a leash on Winnie to lead her to the garage. We took my Jeep Grand Cherokee for the space. The chatter was pretty steady between Rebecca and me as Trick sat silently, picking at his cuticles. The closer we got to my parents' home, the pickier he became. Manayunk was quiet. Most people were cooking and getting ready for guests. When we parked in front of the brick rowhouse, he was chewing his lower lip.

I reached over to give his knee a squeeze. His gaze flew to me. "They are going to love you just as much as I do," I softly said. His smile was shaky.

"Aww, you two are so cute." Rebecca. Right. I'd nearly forgotten about her in the back seat; I'd been so lost in Trick's eyes. Yeah, I had it bad. "Your parents' house is so cute."

I patted Trick's leg, then turned off the engine. "It's small, but it's home."

Winnie led the way, yipping in excitement when we entered the house. I breathed in the rich aroma of roasting turkey, sage, and cinnamon. I barely had my coat off when my brother Stevie came barreling around the corner—hair Army-short and wearing jeans and a gaudy Hawaiian shirt. I gave him the biggest hug I could.

"Man, you look like you grew another foot," I teased my middle sibling.

"Well, I didn't. Maybe you're shrinking, old man,"

Stevie fired back as we hugged it out. I was so happy he could make it home for a week. His CO had been very accommodating with tweaking block leave for him to fly home. We'd probably not see him at Christmas, but who knew. Maybe we could all fly out after the season was over to lounge on those white Hawaiian beaches. Maybe Trick could come with us. Maybe we would both be out and could hold hands as we walked along enjoying the tropical breeze on our faces...

Speaking of Trick. "Hey, this is my special friend, Trick." I pulled back in time to see the rest of the Fulkowski clan pushing into the tiny foyer. "And his sister, Rebecca." Winnie barked. "You all know this attention hound," I chuckled, then lifted the dog from the floor so she could wash everyone's faces.

Even though my family knew Trick and I were involved, we had agreed to keep things on the downlow and be cautious. As much as we hated it, the press did know where my family lived. They'd pestered my parents, my brothers, and even the neighbors. I didn't doubt that someone could be lurking around outside trying to peek in and catch me and Trick doing I don't know what. Fucking on my mother's futon? It was a crummy way to live, but until things were all out in the open, we'd be extremely careful the moment we left the security of my home.

Joey seemed to be stapled to Rebecca's side for the rest of the day. Larry and Trick fell into a long discussion about baseball—a sport that Trick enjoyed watching. Mom and Dad flittered about, ensuring we all ate our fill and then some. Mom kept putting more gravy on Trick's stuffing and adding extra dollops of whipped cream to his slices—yes slices—of pumpkin pie. Larry took note of the preferential treatment and made a comment.

"When you bring a special friend to dinner, I'll give them extra whippy too," Mom parried, which made us all laugh.

Trick was stuffed to the gills and seemed to be about as relaxed as I had ever seen him. I sat back as I sipped my mother's amazing coffee—mine never tasted this good— and simply enjoyed seeing him interacting with my brothers and parents. He'd never had this in his life, this stupidly loud brothers and sisters and adults and yapping dog sort of bedlam over a table cluttered with dirty dishes and a wishbone set aside for drying and future wishes. I wished I could have changed that for him. We'd both lost our mothers far too young, but I had come here. Trick had been flung into a fucking conversion camp. No warm hugs from a loving father, no younger siblings to care for, no motherly embraces in the night when the nightmares came creeping in. Just cold, harsh hatred. I wasn't a religious man, but I prayed I never met Pastor Harrington. If I did, I might have to beat him into pudding for what he had done to his son. As I didn't wish to go to jail for battering a clergyman, it was for the best if his path and mine never crossed.

"Okay, so who's taking Dallas?" Dad asked before pushing out of his seat with a groan, then waving us all into the kitchen. Mom sat smiling, tired but glowing, as we all started cleaning up around her. She would sit there sipping coffee and nibbling on pie with our guests while we loaded the dishwasher. And wiped the counters, and swept the floor, and made sure her kitchen was as spotless as she always left it.

Football talk filled the kitchen as cleanup got underway. Cookie bets and more coffee were made. I peeked around the corner of the kitchen into the small dining room. Rebecca and my mother were talking about college classes, while Trick poked at his pie crust with his fork.

"If you don't like crust, you don't have to eat it," Mom said, then gave Trick a smile that he returned awkwardly.

"Loser. I love crust!" Rebecca grabbed the crust up, shoved it into her mouth, and then giggled, sending crumbs down the front of her. All three at the table laughed. Honest laughter, rich and warm, bubbled out of Trick. Winnie danced around them hoping for bigger bits of pie crust to drop to the carpet.

Dad hooked an arm around my shoulder. I glanced to the side to see what I would look like in twenty years. Some silver hair, a little softer around the middle, and some well-earned laugh lines.

"You really like him, don't you?" Dad asked as my dog put on a show that had Trick, Mom, and Rebecca clapping along as Winnie did her feed-me-I'm-so-hungry two-step.

"I love him, Dad," I whispered over the din of my brothers arguing about which type of shoelace was best. Honestly, the three of them could bicker about the dumbest things. I kind of loved it. Pretty soon someone would be in a headlock. It was inevitable.

"I can tell." He gave the nape of my neck a squeeze, then turned to yell at the other guys to stop messing around before they broke something.

Trick glanced my way when something in the kitchen clattered to the floor. His gaze met mine, and I saw contentment in his eyes. I mouthed "I love you" to him. He mouthed it back. Then, my brother Joey came charging out of the kitchen as my middle brother was trying to slap a stranglehold on him. The other ape sibling cheered them on as Dad tossed out dire warnings about busting up Mom's knickknacks.

Called it.

WINNIE PADDED DOWN THE STAIRS TO JOIN US AFTER checking in on Rebecca.

Trick was tucked under my arm on the sofa, a small fire was burning in the fireplace, and a light snow was falling. Winter was paying us all kinds of attention of late. I had to wonder if that meant we'd have a bad one.

"I think your sister has stolen my dog's heart," I said as the sad little cocker sat down by my foot and whimpered. "Sorry, girl, but she closed the door for privacy. You'll have to make do with us."

I patted the special blankie she slept on. With a great sigh she leapt up to begrudgingly sleep at my side.

"My sister is pretty cool," Trick said as a log snapped in the hearth.

"She is, and smart as a whip. I'm glad you two found each other. Siblings can be really annoying, but they're also always there if you need them."

I snugged him closer, sighing much like my dog but for a wholly different reason. I was not put out at all. I was in my frigging element. I was home, my belly was full, and I had a man I adored tucked into my side. Snow was falling outside, the fire was crackling, and all was right with the world, at least for this small moment in time.

"I'm seeing that. Your brothers are wild but funny."

I chuckled. "You should have been in that house when we were all living there. It was total chaos. Sports equipment everywhere, toys scattered over the yard, four bikes tossed in the driveway. Boys coming and going, mud, dirt, barking dogs. All packed into that small rowhouse. I often wonder now how my folks didn't go insane amid all that bedlam, but they loved it. Mom says that now that it's only the baby left at home, and he's out most of the time, the house is too quiet."

"Your stepmother is amazing. And your father too. I've never… well, you know, never had a day like that. Shame you lost all your cookies on the football game." He pecked my cheek.

I heaved a sad breath. "Yeah, I should never have bet on New York. Cost me that whole box of sand tarts."

He patted my full belly. "Looks like you can skip a few cookies. You wouldn't have been able to chase down those speedy running backs on Sunday if you'd have brought them home."

"Are you insinuating I'm too old and fat to catch a young, fast athlete?" I bristled playfully. He was probably right. A box of Mom's sand tarts would have sunk me. I'd be running extra miles tomorrow as it was to burn off the stuffing and taters I'd eaten today.

"Well, if the pudge fits," he tossed out, then quick as a flash leapt to his feet and sprinted up the stairs.

"Oh, fuck me," I groaned, heaved my ass up, and thundered up the stairs after him. He was in my bedroom when I found him, easing his shirt over his shoulders all come hither.

"You think you have enough energy to let me suck your brains out through your cock, or do you want to take your Geritol, then watch some *Matlock*?"

Smart ass. I fucking loved that about him. Well, that and a few hundred other things.

"I think I can handle what you can dish out, whippersnapper."

He tossed his shirt to the bed, then gave the zipper on his pants a sharp tug down. "We'll see, Gramps."

I closed the door gently while smiling like a fool.

We'd see who could handle who.

Dear Lord, please don't let me peter out first. Amen. Old but still feisty Tom.

NINETEEN

Trick

I'D TOLD MY LAWYERS I'D LET THEM HANDLE EVERYTHING and stay away from Pastor Cole, but I lied.

Tom didn't say much on the drive—just kept one hand on the wheel and the other close enough to touch me when my knee bounced too hard or I cracked my knuckles too loudly. My stomach rolled the closer we got; a low thrum of nausea lodged beneath my ribs. I kept flashing back to that final sermon—his voice booming as he preached about sin and discipline while I stood backstage, shaking, sixteen and terrified. My palms were damp, my jaw clenched so tight I could hear my teeth grinding.

Rebecca rode in the back, phone in one hand, thumb flying over the screen as she curated some musical journey she called "*Holy Shit Showdown.*" Primarily indie rock, with a dash of angry country for spice. She was trying to distract me. It almost worked. I hadn't wanted her to come. I hadn't wanted Tom here either, but when I announced I was doing this, they'd shadowed me as if I might steal away in the middle of the night.

Atlanta blurred past the window. All the polished glass and streets I remembered from before, and when I saw a sign for the Phantoms arena, it felt surreal. It had only been four, maybe five months, since I'd left, but I'd changed, and I expected the city I'd left behind to have become something different.

"I owe them an apology," I murmured.

"Who?" Tom asked, and I sighed.

"My old team. I self-destructed because it was the only way I knew how, and shit, all I wanted to do was leave Georgia, and I made myself so unlikeable, so damaged…"

"You should send them a fruit basket," Rebecca deadpanned and patted my shoulder.

Something about having her here made me smile. Despite my worries, she was part of my life now, and my father could do something to get to her, ruin her. She said she didn't give a shit, happy with college, with a boyfriend called Colin, who was probably still recovering from my speech about what I'd do if he hurt my sister. Poor bastard because he had Tom backing me up.

She forgave me, though—said she was so happy to have a big brother—and at first, I couldn't believe her, so deep in denial I could ever be someone who was a good person to know. I'd unpicked a lot since November, and with Christmas only a week away, I felt I could take on the world. Telling the Railers my truth was step one. Noah being right there beside me… a friend… and this morning, Cap gave a speech, and the rest of the team smiled and hugged me.

He talked about not listening to social media noise, about the clickbait shit that would be out there, and we all knew he was talking from experience. His divorce was final, his marriage gone, and it had been beaten to death, *everywhere*.

Still, he was the best at what he did, and somehow he led us to good things on the ice. We were at the top of our division now with room to spare, and from the next game against the LA Storm, Noah was moving to my wing for a trial, which he didn't know yet, and I couldn't wait for the coach to tell him.

Yes, Tom and I were a secret for now, tucked away behind closed doors *and* careful glances, but Tom's love—quiet, constant, and fiercely loyal—had become my anchor. He didn't just make me smile; he reminded me how to want happiness again. Whenever he pulled a laugh from me, it chipped away at the thick armor I'd built around myself. What he gave me wasn't loud or showy, but it was steady, and it lit a fire in the dark corners I'd long forgotten. For the first time, I felt seen. Loved. Safe.

But as soon as the Temple of the Radiant Truth compound came into sight—those white towers rising like a false promise, ostentatious and gleaming, a twisted parody of a church—my gut twisted into knots. It wasn't only the architecture, all gleam and grandeur with nothing real underneath. It was a memory, thick in my throat. That place had shaped me, broken me, convinced me that I was less-than unless I was exactly what they demanded. Seeing it again made my skin itch, my hands clench. It was like staring down a lie.

"Sure you want to do this, babe?" Tom asked as the gates loomed.

No. But I had to.

I stepped out alone.

Only, I wasn't alone for long. Rebecca, cap pulled low and eyes sharp with purpose, climbed out and came straight to my side. She gripped my hand—tight, defiant—and I opened my mouth to tell her to get back in the car, to stay out of this, even threw Tom a look, but all he did was shrug. Rebecca knew her mind, and I guess I was lucky that Tom had agreed to back off and not go in with me. Bec stared at me with a stubborn tilt to her chin, and I knew I was wasting my breath.

"Don't say anything," I warned, low. "You don't know him—"

"He doesn't know *me*," she shot back, so damn fierce.

There was fire in her—more than I'd ever had—and suddenly, it felt as though the roles had been reversed. As though she was the protector now. The strong one. The one who could keep *me* from breaking.

Security saw me coming. There were big gates and a bigger camera. I stood before the lens, and it clicked once; no one said a word. Access was granted. The prodigal son had returned.

The gate buzzed open, and I walked through with as much confidence as I could find. The building hadn't changed;, all white stone and gold trim. Motivational scripture was painted ten feet high along the outer walls—salvation for sinners and discipline for the wayward. Every image came with a QR code to donate. Inside, it smelled like beeswax polish and judgment, and I headed straight past security, Rebecca gripping my hand, sending out a cheery morning to the woman at the desk.

The receptionist blinked as we passed. "Wait! You need a security pass—"

We didn't stop.

My footsteps echoed in the vaulted hallway, and the doors to the inner sanctum were exactly where I remembered. I pushed through, and there he was.

Cole Harrington II. Pastor Cole. Preacher. CEO of salvation—if you paid him enough.

He looked older. Fewer lines on his face than I expected, but the weight in his stare was the same—dense, heavy, like standing in front of a storm that hadn't yet broken. My breath caught. A pulse of heat rose behind my eyes, that old instinct to shrink back, to disappear. The air between us thickened, and I swore I could still smell the cologne he used when I was a kid, sharp and cloying, tied to sermons and punishments. My heart pounded so hard it felt as if it echoed in my ribs.

"Cole," he said. Not Trick. Never Trick. Then, he glanced at Rebecca, rolling his eyes. "Always the drama with you, son."

"Hi, sperm donor," Rebecca chirped, her voice dripping with sarcasm.

I tightened my grip to warn her, as the pastor's lips thinned. What I wouldn't give to have Tom defending us right now with his muscles and his bulk. I imagined him taking down Pastor Cole, forcing his face into the carpet, and crowing about how he'd freed everyone else to run. A bubble of hysterical laughter forced its way out, and my father swung his gaze to me.

He pressed the button on his intercom. "Get Sawyer in here," he barked. The lawyer.

It had always struck me that Lawyer Sawyer should have chosen a profession that didn't rhyme with his name, and yet another bubble of laughter tried to escape. I needed to be levelheaded, not hysterical. The side door opened, and Sawyer walked in—slick, smarmy, white suit, the whole thing—and he hovered at my dad's right hand. That was some symbolic shit right there, and seriously, I needed to calm the fuck down with wanting to laugh.

"Out with it then," Pastor Cole said.

I tossed the envelope onto his desk—my own symbolic gesture—because by now, Tom would've alerted my lawyer, and every document would already be in his inbox.

"You're not getting any more money from me," I said. "I'm not a revenue stream. And I'm done."

He didn't flinch, raised an eyebrow, and glanced from me to Rebecca. "Is this her doing?"

"No."

"You know she's trying to blackmail you, ruin you, make you less than I made you."

Now, it was her turn to squeeze my hand.

"No, you were the one who blackmailed me and ruined me, *Pastor Cole*." I couldn't call him *Father*; he wasn't my *dad*. He was nothing.

"Prone to hysterics, just like your mother," he told Sawyer, who smirked. Then Pastor Cole sat back in his chair, grinned at me, feral and smug, as though he held all the cards and was about to lay down a royal flush. The kind of grin that knew secrets and loved how much it hurt to keep them. Self-satisfied and cruel, it was the smile of a man who'd never been told no and didn't plan to start now.

He picked up the envelope and tossed it to Sawyer who fumbled the catch.

"Ungrateful," he spat, standing now, voice taking on that slow, rising cadence he used at the pulpit. "I raised you. I made you into something. And this—this betrayal? For what? Lust? Sin wrapped up in rainbow flags and deviance. Don't think the world will hold your hand, son. They'll spit you out just like Sodom burned. I gave you purpose, and you traded it for corruption. You were meant to return to us and serve the Lord, not defile His design with your perversions."

"Stop." I stepped forward, wishing there wasn't a desk between us. "You don't get to twist this. You want to talk scripture? Fine. Start with 'Fathers, do not embitter your children, or they will become discouraged.' And how about, 'Husbands, be faithful to your wives'? Because I know what you did with Rebecca's mom. Don't pretend this is about righteousness when it's always been about control."

He sneered. "You quote as if you know the Word better than I."

"No," I said. "I quote as someone who's done living afraid of it. I know enough to recognize when love is real and when it's just a weapon."

It had become a battle of scripture—me flinging lines about love, truth, honesty, and forgiveness. He countered with fire, wrath, and damnation. We could've done it for hours. Days. Years. And I would've kept standing there, hurling truth like stones, until he finally looked at me and saw something he couldn't deny.

Me. Whole. Unashamed. Loved.

"I'm not for sale anymore," I snapped. "I'm gay. I'm coming out." Wow, that was the first time I'd said that, and the words felt right.

Rebecca leaned into me. "You are?

"I love him, Bec," I said, using the nickname I'd given her in my head for the first time out loud.

"Ah, yes." Pastor Cole sneered. "Thomas Fulkowski, the football player." He plucked a sheet of paper from his desk and held it up with deliberate care. "National security number, social media logins, his old college transcript—even his gym schedule. You think your pretend-love makes you untouchable, son? I've known how to break people longer than you've been breathing."

My temper cracked wide open. "Touch him and…" and what? Touch him and die? Right now, I could leap over the desk and strangle the man who'd raised me with so much hate and self-loathing.

"And what, son?" he said.

"And *nothing*," I said, and he grinned again.

"Good boy," he said. "Now, if that's all."

"No, you don't get it. Nothing—because I don't *need* to do anything for you anymore," I said, voice rising with every word. "You threatened to lock me away, to convert me until I signed that damn contract at sixteen. You told me you'd lie about Mom—say she took her own life—to scare me into obedience. And I believed you could do that. But the thing is, we have the truth now. Proof Mom had cancer, proof you faked her healing with your bullshit sermons. A letter from her surgeon. Testimony from Rebecca's mother, showing exactly how faithful you weren't. And I don't care if you sneer or dismiss me—I'm not that scared kid anymore. I'm not your puppet. Oh, and that envelope? That's the new contract. I don't owe you a single cent. You stay out of my life, and you keep my mom's name out of your sermons. She loved me. She didn't leave me because she wanted to. She left because she didn't have a choice. And now? I *do*. I'm done." My chest hurt when I drew in a breath, because that had all spilled out in one go.

Pastor Cole's jaw twitched. A flicker of something crossed his face—concern, maybe, a blink-and-you-miss-it hesitation—but it was gone just as quickly. He gave the faintest nod toward Sawyer, who moved closer and retrieved the envelope. "Again, nothing but hysterics."

"My mom was kind and sweet, I remember that."

"She was nothing, and I gave you everything. Structure. Purpose.

"No. You had a product. And I'm not for sale anymore."

"Pastor," Sawyer began, "this is something you should see." He passed the papers to my dad, who pushed them away.

"That's your job."

"He's threatening to sue the church," Sawyer said, eyes flicking between the paper and Pastor Cole, "for fraud, emotional abuse, unlawful emancipation, and misappropriation of charitable funds. There's testimony, digital records, and a forensic accountant's report. This isn't just a PR issue. This is federal."

"You're threatening me, boy?" he spat, voice rising with the fury of the pulpit. The air crackled with his righteous indignation, as if hellfire would rain down at his command. "I am the vessel of the Lord! I *saved* you from the filth, from temptation! I bled for your soul. I *burned* for your salvation! And this is how you repay me? With slander and betrayal? Woe unto those who rise against the chosen!"

That was the moment the laughter escaped for real, but it turned into a choked sob, and Rebecca stepped in front of me, this tiny slip of a girl getting between me and a man full of hate.

"It's not a threat," she said.

Pastor Cole blinked, stunned that she'd dared to speak. His gaze snapped to her like the crack of a whip, mouth twitching in disgust. "The girl thinks she has a voice now," he sneered. "You don't even know the rules of the world you've stepped into. Keep talking, and you'll learn just how quickly that freedom you cling to can be taken away."

I pushed her behind me—this was a big brother's job now. "It's not a threat because the papers have just been filed. Your entire ministry was built on sand, and the authorities have just started digging."

I turned to leave, ushering Rebecca before me.

"You can't do this," he snapped, voice cracking with fury. "You'll destroy me."

He stepped forward, hand raised as if to call down some righteous fury.

"God will judge you for this! You think you can go against what I teach, but you've been led astray. Love the sinner, hate the sin—" His voice wavered, losing steam. "You were my son. I gave you everything. You owe me! I love you, son. I can forgive you."

"I don't owe you a fucking thing," I snapped. "And

your love is destructive, and I don't want your forgiveness, old man!"

His mask slipped.

"This—this ministry—it supports thousands, it feeds the flock, it feeds me—do you have any idea what you've done?"

"Chosen love."

"You're choosing him over God. Over me." He was unraveling now, flipping between wrath and despair. He staggered back a step, mouth slack with disbelief. "They'll take the houses. The cars. The donations are already drying up. You've... you've ruined me."

Not the church, not his beliefs, but I'd ruined him? That sounded about right.

I opened the door, waited for Rebecca to step outside, then turned back to the man who'd tried to chain me and shook my head.

"I'm walking away to start a life with the man I love. I'm done."

We walked out, head high, but heart broken, and tears made my throat tight. Rebecca held my hand again and hugged me as soon as the gates closed. "I'm so proud of you, big brother."

"You and I are going to have words about you coming in with me," I warned without heat, and she hugged me harder with a laugh. "But thank you, Bec. Thank you."

Behind us, Tom waited with the engine running. Rebecca's playlist was still playing—some folksy anthem about burning bridges and dancing in the ashes.

Seemed appropriate.

COMING OUT WAS ALMOST ANTICLIMACTIC. YES, IT changed my world. Yes, there was blowback. I got hate, I lost endorsements, and some fans walked away. But I also got love. Real love. And Tom was right there through all of it, hand in mine, unwavering.

Layton had arranged a press conference. We'd been prepared for pushback, for questions and chaos, but everything changed before the mic was even turned on. News had already broken about the Temple of the Radiant Truth Ministry. Pastor Cole had been arrested at the start of the week—fraud, abuse, conspiracy. The headlines wrote themselves.

Reporters barely wanted to ask about me. The spotlight had shifted entirely to what I'd seen and done inside the ministry, and for once, I was okay with that being everyone's focus. I wasn't the scandal anymore. I was only a man standing beside the one he loved.

The man who was sitting at the glass right behind the bench for our game against the LA Storm. Management had offered him a spot in the team VIP area, but nope, my man wanted to be down with the fans, cheering me on.

Coming out hadn't cost me everything. In fact, once the storm had passed, I realized how much more I'd gained. Love. Truth. Freedom.

And hockey. God, I loved hockey again.

The buzzer still echoed off the glass when I skated toward Noah, adrenaline pumping. We'd just pulled off the move we'd practiced in warmup—a no-look behind-the-back pass from him to me as we crossed the blue line. The puck kissed my blade and flew off like a missile, slicing into the top corner with half a second on the clock.

Chaos exploded around us—helmets tossed, gloves in the air, the bench clearing. I threw my arms around Noah, who was laughing so hard he nearly fell over. The whole arena erupted. My teammates mobbed me, but I only had eyes for Rebecca jumping up and down, and Tom, who was out of his seat, both fists in the air, shouting something I couldn't hear but felt in my bones.

We'd won the game. We were top of the division. And I was on fire.

The Storm's Cameron Chavkin skated past us, stick tapping the ice, grinning despite the loss. "Damn, Trick, that was beautiful. You part of the Rainbow Hockey Alliance now?"

"Wait, is that a thing?" I shot back, still catching my breath.

"Consider yourself signed up," he quipped, offering a fist bump I returned without hesitation.

My teammates piled on. Coach looked like he might actually smile for once. We were top of the division. I'd buried a game-winner with the man I loved watching from the stands, and Noah, who was fast becoming my best friend, was on my wing.

This was everything.

I loved hockey. I loved Tom. And for the first time in my life, I loved *me*.

Epilogue

TOM

THERE'S AN OLD SAYING ABOUT HOW GOD MOVES IN mysterious ways.

As I sat in the locker room of the BoltFuel Stadium in Atlanta, waiting for Coach to arrive for one last pep talk, fully geared up, fifteen minutes before we took to the field to meet the San Francisco Stars, I couldn't help but smile at how Trick had come full circle. He was out in the stands with my entire family plus his sister, Noah and Brody, living it up. How opportune that the NHL had their All-Star week lined up to coincide—not on purpose, I assumed —with the Super Bowl. Not saying that hockey knew it couldn't compete with football buuuuuut…

My man had left Georgia in disgrace and had come home a hero of sorts. He was certainly heroic in my eyes, and the eyes of many young gay kids who had heard his story and could see that there was a way out. I could never express how proud I was of him. Coming out took balls. Standing up to the person who had made your life a living hell was beyond ballsy. It was next-level valiant.

"Hey."

I looked up from my cleats, an old Phil Collins song flowing into my ears, to see Tucker standing in front of me. Great. This was not the vibe I needed before hitting the field to play my last game for all the fucking marbles. I sighed, then tugged a bud out.

"Look, if you're here to empty your chamber pot of judgmental hate over my head you can just haul your ass right back to the other side of the room," I growled softly.

Ty, sitting a few feet over and lost in his pregame meditation, blinked an eye open to watch what was going on.

"No, nothing like that. I just wanted to apologize."

Sure I wasn't hearing correctly, I yanked the other bud out just as that killer drum bit was breaking free. "Am I being pranked?"

"No, man, no, I just…" He glanced around the room, then sank to one knee beside me. Others were watching now. Mostly observing and gauging the vibe. No one wanted to be stressed before the game started. And no one wanted any bullshit. "My sister has some kids. One of them just came out as a lesbian."

Oh. Okay. Yep. That was cool for her. Brave kid. I bit down on my tongue to stop myself from being that guy. The guy who mentioned how people suddenly sang a different tune when something impacted them personally.

"You must be proud of her for speaking her truth," I said instead of being a jerk. But man did I long to be jerky.

"Yeah, well, it was a shock. But we're all trying our best to be supportive. She's a good girl, smart, going to college in the fall to be a nurse."

"She sounds amazing."

He shifted uncomfortably, the overhead lights reflecting off his bald head. "She's my favorite niece." He met my gaze for the first time in months. "I see now that I was wrong about you, and your boyfriend, about a lot. I know I can't take back what was said, but I would like to say I'm sorry for spitting at you. That was crass."

"Yeah, it was." I sat back, drew in a breath, and offered him my wrapped hand. "I accept your apology. I don't know as we'll ever be besties, but I hope I can dump some champagne over your thick skull after we win that pretty silver trophy."

"I'd like that too. God bless you, Tom, for your forgiving heart."

We shook. He ambled off. Ty gave me a quirked brow. Coach arrived. We all went silent as he said a quick non-denominational prayer before launching into a short, but fiery, speech about our character, what our legacy was, and how important this moment was. He spoke of teamwork, how we would not settle for second, and how each of us will carry the memory of this game with us our entire lives. Then, with a nod from our captain, we rose and lined up in the tunnel. Energy was high. Men were bouncing, shouting, some were still praying. I was rocking back and forth, inhaling the smell of AstroTurf, sweat, and excitement.

"Hey, man, we took a vote. You lead us out," Ty shouted at me. I gawked at my friend, then glanced around at the other players in gold and blue. They all nodded. "It's your last game, man. You take us out."

"Shit." I choked up, then nodded. Taking a deep

breath, I moved to the front of the pack and heard the stadium announcer leading up to our exit. With a rush of adrenalin, my old knees felt like those of a twenty-year-old as I charged out of the tunnel. The crowd went wild. Well, half the crowd. We ran past two huge foam pumas that blew smoke, then between twin lines of our team cheerleaders and our mascot, a dude in a puma suit, charging around making clawing motions at the opposing team.

Things went quickly then. Almost as if time were speeding up when I wanted it to slow down. I needed to relish every moment of this game. It was my last. That made me feel far too many things, so I pushed the emotions down for now. I'd sort them all out later. We bided our time until the flyover and anthem were sung, then we met for the coin toss.

We won the flip. We deferred to the second half, which meant the Stars would receive the ball first. This half. Coach liked us having the first possession in the second.

Feeling our oats, the defense took to the field with me shouting at the rest of the mountainous men to take him down. We all knew who he was. Gerome Ivans, the quarterback of the Stars. Great player, nice guy, cute wife and kid. I planned to smash his face into the green as often as I could. It was nothing personal. Just my job. Dropping down into my stance, I felt the love flowing to me from Trick. Somewhere up there, amid seventy thousand fans, was my boyfriend. Maybe I was being a little silly, but hey, a man in love is allowed to be giddy now and again.

Knuckles on the turf, heart pounding, I zeroed in on

Gerome behind his offensive line. We wanted to make an impression right out of the gate. Gerome's audible was hard to pick up with the crowd noise, but I caught the movement of his foot as he shifted.

The ball was snapped, and we surged. Bodies hit bodies, men grasping at other men, the grunt of impact. A small hole opened up, and I blew through it on the left as Tucker came at Gerome from the right. Pressured right from the snap, Gerome faded back, turned, and tried to fake a pass to his wide receiver, who was obviously not open because he then tried to rush the ball. I dove at his legs to take him down. We'd barely hit the turf when I was yanked to my feet and beat on the helmet by Tucker. I threw a fist into the air.

Impression made.

We played hard, crushing the Stars with a defensive squad that their offense could not slow. Exhausted and soaked in sweat, we were up 35–14 with two minutes left in the third when Tyrese did what he does best. Second and seventeen, he found himself under some pressure from the Stars defense and jogged to his right. Spying his fave receiver, Jolie Biggs, open along the sidelines, Ty passed the ball. Jolie leapt into the air, caught it, then juked around two Stars defenders to sprint down the field to score. I took that as a sign.

The fourth quarter was all Pumas. I got my fingertips on a wobbly shuttle from Gerome. The tip sent the ball into the belly of one of my defensive linemen who fell on it, then jumped up to hold the fumbled ball over his head. That sealed the fate of the Stars, although I'd sensed they were done from that first play when I'd smooshed Gerome's face into the dirt.

The fans grew louder and louder as Ty began taking a knee with less than a minute left in the fourth. When there were fifteen seconds left, we dumped a cooler of energy drink over Coach's head as was tradition. He sputtered and laughed as the clock ran out. I hugged Coach. I hugged Tucker. I hugged a cameraman. Shit, I was crying and laughing and embracing every damn person who came near me. The crush after the final fireworks was stifling, to say the least. With all the celebrations that followed that decisive win, I could only think of how nice it would be to have Trick down here with me.

Reporters pushed in around us, many asking how we felt. Like, seriously, what a dumb question. We felt great! We were the champs. We had spiffy new hats on our sweaty heads that even said so. While I was chatting with a pretty lady reporter, she gave me a wink and asked what is usually asked of the MVP, which was Tyrese. Ty totally earned that recognition, but a nod to the D wouldn't have gone amiss voting fans and media panel. Just saying.

"What do you plan to do after the Super Bowl?" she shouted as she glanced up at me.

I stared into the camera and gave the biggest shit-eating grin I had.

"I'm going to Hawaii with my boyfriend!" I hoped Trick was watching the interview.

Turned out he had seen my face on the scoreboard telling the world my plans. I knew that because he wiggled into the locker room after the win, smiling, looking about as good as any man I had ever seen before. Just as the other guys squeezed and kissed their wives, I pulled Trick into my arms, kissed him soundly, then poured champagne over his head. My family piled in as well, shouting and whooping it up in true Fulkowski style. Mom was crying, which was so very much my stepmother. She would be a wreck when her boys got married.

He coughed as he wiped bubbly from his lashes.

"I owe you a dousing when we win the Cup," he sputtered, and I agreed to that without question.

He could dump fizzy drink over me whenever he wanted. I'd be there for his wins and his losses for as long as he wanted me at his side. I was going nowhere. Well, that was a lie, I *was* going somewhere, and he was coming with me…

I'D SEEN A LOT OF BEAUTIFUL THINGS IN MY LIFE, BUT nothing could compare with the light of a pink Kauai sunset on Trick's whiskery cheeks. I couldn't take my eyes off him as he lounged on the sand, his toes in the surf. He was a changed man. Totally. And I loved that I had been there to watch him rise from the ashes of his past like a glorious phoenix. He smiled now, a lot, and laughed a lot, and was finding his path in life as a queer man. Openly queer and so damn proud of himself.

"I can feel you staring at me." He lay spread out on the beach of our private little romantic rental. It had cost us nothing as it belonged to a rapper friend of his. So, we had left the family behind after a week on Oahu, then flown here to do a week of nothing but hike, swim, and have sex.

Trick was chill as a cucumber, his spirits high even though the Railers had been knocked out in the second round of the playoffs. He'd been down for a few days, but knew in his heart of hearts, they'd be back stronger and tougher next season. I knew it as well.

I did not rub my shiny new championship ring under his nose. Much. He'd get his. Besides, I had a different kind of ring I wanted to show him, and it had nothing to do with sports. But not now. It was too soon.

"You're pretty, I can't help it." I ran my hand down Winnie's back as we relaxed on a chaise lounge while the palm trees swayed and huffed as Wink rolled on his back to get some sun on his belly. I immediately covered his soft bits with a towel and scooted him in the shade. Trick had adopted the one-eyed sweetheart just before Christmas, a few days after confronting Pastor Cole. He said Wink deserved a good home and told me that he knew he was a good person.

It was a turning point.

The moment Trick accepted he was good and right and loved.

So, our family of him, me, and Winnie, now included Wink. Not forgetting Rebecca, who was another constant in my man's life.

"I like it here. They got any hockey teams you could ask to be traded to. No snow. That would make you happy. And all the pineapple you can eat."

He'd eaten far too much pineapple for one man in the past ten days.

"I don't think they have a pro team." He yawned and stretched, arms over his head. I drank in all that pale flesh bathed in flamingo tones. "Besides, I like it in Harrisburg. I'm feeling it there, you know?"

"I know." And I did. He and the team were gelling slowly. He was happy. And no matter how much I loved this island, I didn't want to mar his happiness by being greedy. "I'm going to sell my place in Jersey and buy a summer home here." He rolled his head to study me through his spiffy shades. "I'm serious. I don't want to be in Jersey. That's too far for you to travel during the season. I want us to be together."

"Like live together?" he asked. I nodded. Winnie licked my fingers, so I resumed petting the princess. "That's... big."

"I know. Does it scare you?"

He went back to looking skyward. I wasn't sure if his eyes were open or not. From down the beach, the soft sounds of a local band filled the warm air. We'd spent a few nights at the Seabird's Song having dinner and listening to the native musicians. Seriously, this place was paradise. I know that was said about the islands all the time, but it is the absolute truth.

"Not really. Scared is strong. I was scared of my father."

Not anymore though. Big Daddy Pastor Man was in prison with no bail as he was a huge flight risk, all his assets had been seized, and I for one was happier than a seagull with a French fry. I'd done my best to not get riled up as the legal proceedings began, but patience wasn't always my strongest suit. Justice for Trick could not come soon enough.

"It's just a big step." He rolled to his side, the towel

under him wadding up as he moved to his hip and rested his head in his hand. "Are you so sure you want to do something like that with me? I'm not the most stable guy."

"Stop that. That's your father talking. You're the most steady man I know. And I love you and want to be with you, and Winnie wants a house with you in it too."

That made him chuckle. "The dog wants to live with me?"

"For sure. She adores you."

"She is pretty cute." He pushed up from the beach, sand stuck to his long, muscular frame, and came to kneel beside our chaise. "You're not half bad either, even if your knees do pop when you get out of bed."

"Are you insinuating something?"

"No, no, of course not. Just wondering if you'll be able to keep up with me if we do move in together. I'm not sure you're quite up to a younger lover."

"Hey, I can catch men half my age," I reminded him.

He stole a quick, sandy kiss. "Prove it, Gramps."

And off he ran like a rocket.

"Fuck me," I moaned, then hefted myself up and off the chaise. Winnie flew off my lap and was on his heels in a second, barking furiously, making Trick laugh merrily. He sped towards the little bar with the delicious platters filled with Loco Moco and Saimin, with me and my dog in hot pursuit. He let me catch him as the sun sank lower behind the waves.

"Noah's dad might know of some nice places for sale near where he lives. Rumor has it he knows people," Trick whispered after the kiss ended.

"Is that a yes to moving in with me?"

"It's not a no."

I chuckled and kissed him once more. Life with Trick was never going to be easy or boring. I couldn't wait to experience it all with him.

THE END

One jet, two weeks, no regrets.
_____

Coming next in the Railers Legacy series

Powder

One jet, two weeks, no regrets... until the Winter Games change everything.

With age comes wisdom, they say. Jack O'Leary—Cap to his team—isn't sure he's gotten any wiser during his tenure on the Railers, but he has gotten older. Jack is at a loose end after a messy divorce from his high school sweetheart. He's not ready to retire yet, and he's not looking for romance, but fate has other plans. A chance meeting on a flight to a summer getaway that's supposed to be a post-divorce morale booster turns into fourteen days of discovery and wild passion. Tumbling into bed with Knox Wilder was not on his bingo card, but Jack's not complaining. The young snowboarder is vibrant, sexy, and just what Jack needs to rebuild his confidence. After the vacation ends, the two go their separate ways, and Jack returns to the ice and his lonely life. When he's invited to join the US hockey team, he's honored to accept. No sooner is he in Italy than he sees Knox standing in the team's hotel lobby, as unforgettable as ever. Is Jack brave enough to rekindle their affair, or will he return to Harrisburg alone once more?

Fresh off a breakout season and hailed as one of snowboarding's rising stars, Knox Wilder has earned a luxury vacation from a major sponsor, with first-class everything, including flying by private jet. The last thing he expects on the flight is to meet Jack, a quiet, gorgeous NHL legend who is hot as Hades. Jack's older, jaded, and heartbreakingly closed off—but Knox can't stay away. Neither of them is looking for anything serious, but attraction flares, and two weeks of sun and sex sounds perfect—no promises, no pressure, just fun. They part ways and their careers resume. But their fling crashes headfirst into reality when both are selected for Team USA. They're teammates in a pressure cooker of media attention, gold-medal dreams, and emotions that have never entirely cooled. Can they turn their fleeting escape into a second chance at romance—or will fear, fame, and the weight of expectations leave them both out in the cold?

Powder is an age-gap, opposites-attract, second-chance romance set against the backdrop of Olympic glory. Featuring a disheartened hockey veteran, a golden boy snowboarder with something to prove, a post-divorce fling, and a no-strings vacation that turns into something real, just in time for the biggest stage in the world.

Hockey Series' from RJ Scott & V.L. Locey

Harrisburg Railers

Owatonna U Hockey

Arizona Raptors

Boston Rebels

LA Storm

Chesterford Coyotes - Young Adult

Railers Legacy

Rochester Copperheads (AHL, coming soon)

Oxford Knights (coming 2027)

Harrisburg Railers

When hockey wunderkind Tennant Rowe meets his new coach, he knows he's in trouble. Jared Madsen is nine years older than Tennant, impossibly attractive, and — worst of all — his brother's off-limits best friend. Is their chemistry worth the risk?

Changing Lines (Railers 1)

Can Tennant show Jared that age is just a number, and that love is all that matters?

The Rowe Brothers are famous hockey hotshots, but as the youngest of the trio, Tennant has always had to play against his brothers' reputations. To get out of their shadows, and against their advice, he accepts a trade to the Harrisburg Railers, where he runs into Jared Madsen. Mads is an old family friend and his brother's one-time teammate. Mads is Tennant's new coach. And Mads is the sexiest thing he's ever laid eyes on.

Jared Madsen's hockey career was cut short by a fault in his heart, but coaching keeps him close to the game. When Ten is traded to the team, his carefully organized world is thrown into chaos. Nine years his junior and his best friend's brother, he knows Ten is strictly off-limits, but as soon as he sees Ten's moves, on and off the ice, he knows that his heart could get him into trouble again.

––––––––––

Harrisburg Railers (Hockey Romance)

1. Changing Lines
2. First Season
3. Deep Edge
4. Poke Check
5. Last Defense
6. Goal Line
7. Neutral Zone
8. Hat Trick
9. Save The Date
10. Baby Makes Three
11. Rivals
12. Perfect Gifts
13. Family First

––––––––––

Railers Volume 1 | Railers Volume 2 | Railers Volume 3 | Railers Volume 4

Meet the men of Owatonna University's hockey team

Ryker (Owatonna U, 1)

Ryker is hockey royalty, Jacob is a poor country boy. Can two vastly different people find common ground and become the men they want to be?

Ryker comes from a long line of championship-winning hockey players. Playing college hockey to develop his game is his only focus, and nothing will stand in the way of him working to become the best player. He has no room for relationships, people who point out his flaws, or anyone who calls him on his dreams. He certainly has no place for love, and meeting Jacob is nothing but a useful distraction on the side. After all trying to get his Owatonna Eagles teammate into bed is less work and more play. When tragedy rocks his family, his charmed life crumbles, and the only person he can turn to is the same one who claims to hate him.

Jacob Benson has only known hard work and stifling conservative values his whole life. Born and raised in the small rural community of Eden Crossing, Minnesota, he's the only son of a hard-working but struggling dairy farming family. Jacob is using his skills in hockey to finance his way to an agricultural science degree. These four years at Owatonna U. will probably be the only time he has to enjoy life, gain acceptance about his sexuality, and live openly before his inevitable return to the farm. Running into a pretty rich boy like Ryker Madsen is putting a damper on his enjoyment of life away from home. Ryker's flip, conceited, carefree attitude grates on Jacob's every nerve. So why, if Ryker is everything he dislikes, does he want nothing more than to explore the sinful dreams that his annoying teammate stars in every night?

Ryker

———

Owatonna U Hockey (Hockey Romance)

Arizona Raptors

Coast to Coast (Arizona Raptors 1)

Coast To Coast

When opposites attract, this bottom-of-the-league team will never be the same again.

A stipulation in his father's will forces Mark back into the arms of a family that disowned him and leaves him one-third owner of a hockey team facing financial ruin. He doesn't even watch hockey, let alone like it, and wants nothing more than to head back to New York. Then there's the new coach, a stubborn, opinionated, irritating man with superiority issues and questionable music taste. Butting heads with Rowen becomes the new normal, but it comes with passionate debate and an all-consuming lust.

Challenged to rebuild one of the worst teams in the league into a future cup contender, Rowen can't pass up the opportunity. Never in his twenty years of hockey has he ever seen a team managed so badly or coached players overflowing with resentment and bigotry. Yet there's something about this team and this city that compels him to roll up his sleeves and start dismantling. If only Mark, one of three siblings who now own the Raptors, wasn't so damned rock-headed yet so damned appealing his job might be easier. It doesn't look like either is willing to give in, but one night in a dark, desert hotel changes everything.

Coast To Coast

Arizona Raptors (Hockey Romance)

Boston Rebels

Top Shelf (Boston Rebels 1)

Acting on the attraction to his best friend's brother has always been off the table for Xander until a passionate hookup with Mason at a beach resort begins a love affair that burns long after summer ends.

Mason specializes in assisting same-sex couples on their journey to becoming parents and fighting every rule that blocks his way in the stuck-in-the-past agency that hired him. Living in his brother's pool house is rent-free, and every cent he earns he saves for his dream—that one day he'd have his own company helping others. The downside is that he has to see his annoying brother every day, the upside is that his brother's teammates from the

Boston Rebels make regular visits. The eye candy that passes Mason's window is almost enough to make him consider dating a hockey player, but not just any player though. Ever since Xander —his brother's childhood friend—came out as gay at a press conference, Mason's puppy love has turned into a burning attraction he can no longer ignore.

Hockey has been one of Xander's main focuses since he was old enough to balance on skates. Well, hockey and Mason Kingsley, but Mason was always unattainable. Now that he's about to see thirty candles on his birthday cake and is no longer hiding the fact he's gay, he's ready to find a soul mate to make his life complete. A summer vacation is just what he needs to have time to think, but when the Boston Rebels arriving in paradise with Mason in tow, thinking is the last thing he needs. One torrid night under a balmy moon and rules about not messing with his best friend's brother vanish on a warm, tropical breeze.

Summer romances don't generally last past Labor Day, but with the new season about to begin Xander and Mason are going to have to face the world and decide if their love is real enough to withstand everything.

Boston Rebels

Lost In Boston (Free Prequel Novella)

LA Storm

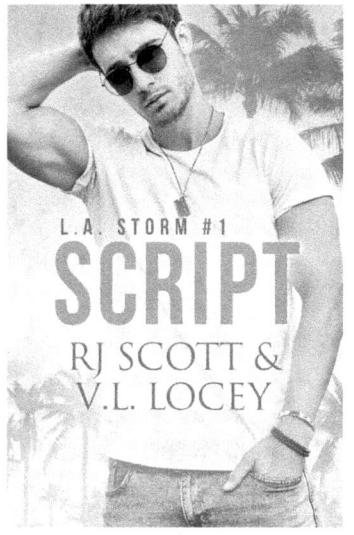

Script (LA Storm, 1)

Script

Hollywood A-lister Finn might be Canadian, but he needs Cameron to show him how to hockey.

Actor Finn Kerrigan is at a crossroads. After growing up a soap star, then starring in a hugely successful trilogy of action movies, he's finally given the chance to read a heartfelt and passionate script that could change his life forever. The role would be enough for people to see him as a serious actor, and maybe even win him an award or two (and no, a golden raspberry award for his action movies doesn't count). Once established as a serious actor he's sure he can come out of the closet and finally live his truth. When he lies to get the part of a hockey player on a struggling team, he suddenly has nowhere to hide. He might be Canadian, but the last time he skated he was ten, and no, he doesn't have hockey in his blood. With only a month until filming starts, he about to be exposed, but partnered with a player who's supposed to be giving him tips, he doesn't realize how many of his secrets will come to light. Falling in lust, one heated kiss at a time, is inevitable, but giving Cameron up at the end of the shoot could break his heart.

Cameron Chavkin is the face of the LA Storm. And the body, and the hair, and the smile. He's at the prime of his career, men and women want to be with him, and he's skating better than he ever has before. His house sits next to a famous rock star's mansion, his garage is filled with expensive cars, and he's even been asked to mentor a once-famous actor in a new hockey movie. Life is pretty sweet. Until the bad boy of hockey meets Finn, a man on the edge with more secrets than Cameron has endorsements. Knowing better than to get involved, Cameron is swept up despite himself, and when it's time to say goodbye to the Storm's most eligible bachelor is finding it hard to follow the script.

Script

LA Storm

Speed (Railers Legacy 1)

Hard ice. Fast cars. Fierce love.

And a race against fate.

Hockey is as natural as breathing for Noah. Growing up with two famous hockey stars as his dads, Noah has always aspired to join the Railers to continue the Lyamin-Gunnarsson legacy. With his degree done, it's time to live that dream, and the first step is being drafted by the team his hall-of-fame dad played for. The second step is to pull on that dusky blue-gray sweater and make his fathers proud. His rookie year is bound to be a season of incredible highs and lows, but one of the biggest highlights is meeting Brody Vance at a fundraiser. Brody is the living epitome of a bad boy hiding his pain behind a devil-may-care attitude. As Noah struggles to keep one eye on the puck and not on Brody, it's only a matter of time before both loves collide in a chaotic splash of media attention.

Bad boy racing driver Brody has spent his life chasing speed and glory and is only points away from his first world championship when a devastating crash ends his season. Determined to make a triumphant comeback, Brody is blindsided by a diagnosis that forces him off the track for good. With his world flipped upside down and family and fans questioning why he left, Brody hides his pain by pushing the limits and refusing to let anyone see the cracks. But after a chance meeting with a sweet, sexy hockey player turns into an unforgettable one-night stand, fate keeps putting Noah in his path. With his heart on the line and his body racing against time, Brody must decide if he's willing to risk it all for love—or if he'll let fear and pride leave him in the dust.

Speed is a steamy M/M romance with a hockey rookie living his family legacy, a bad-boy racing driver with secrets, media attention that would break even the strongest of men, an unforgettable one-night stand, a love that means risking it all, and a hard-won happily ever after.

Railers Legacy

1. *Speed*
2. *Blitz*
3. *Powder*
4. *Fly*

Off The Ice (Chesterford Coyotes, 1)

Off The Ice

A coming-of-age love story with high school, hockey rivalry, friendship, family, and coming out.

Soren's life changes in an instant when he and his younger brother are adopted by hockey royalty. Making sense of his new life is hard enough, but when he's enrolled in a private school it means facing a whole new set of problems. Navigating friendship, family, and hockey is one thing, but being attracted to the boy who vexes him is a whole new thing.

Felix has a reputation to protect. He's the kid who seems to have everything but looks can be deceiving. Spinning lies about his perfect life, he's created a fantasy world that even he has started to believe. Only, it's not long before everything crumbles, all of his pretty lies are revealed, and only his closest rival sees through his pain and stands by him.

Fighting is easy, friendship is hard, but love is everything.

Off The Ice

Chesterford Coyotes

1. Off The Ice
2. On Thin Ice
3. *Dance on Ice*

Free Reads

Please note - in all of these free stories, there will be some spoilers for the main series books.

Railers Short Stories

Volume 1 | Volume 2

LA Storm

Sparkle

The Colts - AHL Short Stories

Pucks & Percentages

Breakaway

Making the Save

Standalone

Waiting for Christmas

Meet RJ Scott

RJ writes MM romance—sometimes sweet, sometimes dark, always with a generous splash of angst and a hint of hurt/comfort.

A born romantic, she's convinced love is love—and every man deserves his happily ever after (especially the ones who swear they don't).

Website - gayromance.co.uk
Newsletter - gayromance.co.uk/mailing-list

Scan for a complete list of ebooks and links.

instagram.com/rjscott_author
amazon.com/author/rj-scott
bookbub.com/authors/rj-scott

Meet V.L. Locey

V.L. Locey loves worn jeans, yoga, belly laughs, walking, reading and writing lusty tales, Greek mythology, the New York Rangers, comic books, and coffee. (Not necessarily in that order.)

She shares her life with her husband, her daughter, one dog, two cats, a flock of assorted domestic fowl, and two Jersey steers.

When not writing spicy romances, she enjoys spending her day with her menagerie in the rolling hills of Pennsylvania with a cup of fresh java in hand.

vllocey.com | vicki@vllocey.com
Newsletter - vllocey.com/newsletter

Scan for a complete list of ebooks and links.

facebook.com/V.L.Locey

x.com/vllocey

instagram.com/vl_locey

bookbub.com/authors/v-l-locey

goodreads.com/vllocey

pinterest.com/vllocey